THE HARBOR OF
LOST SHIPS

THE HARBOR OF LOST SHIPS

BOOK 2

BETHANY SHEHORN

THE HARBOR OF LOST SHIPS
BOOK 2

iUniverse books may be ordered through booksellers or by contacting:

iUniverse
1663 Liberty Drive
Bloomington, IN 47403
www.iuniverse.com
1-800-Authors (1-800-288-4677)

ISBN: 978-1-5320-2490-0 (sc)
ISBN: 978-1-5320-2491-7 (e)

Library of Congress Control Number: 2017910882

Print information available on the last page.

iUniverse rev. date: 08/23/2017

Special thanks to Lea Lindstrom for giving so much of yourself to aid in my growth. You pushed me to be better and granted me the tools to rise. You are amazing and I am forever grateful to have you for a friend.

PART 1

Cause and Effect

CHAPTER 1
The Aftermath

TIME CHANGES US. IT ALWAYS will. People, events, and actions, or lack thereof, all set change in motion.

Liv had left her beloved job at the paper, to the dismay of her boss, Larry, following her wedding to Wes on earth. Since she had been kidnapped and taken to Torr, where Wes had died in her place, but Liv's tears had resurrected him. The devastation of recent events and the massive responsibility of being solely charged with taking down a dark queen in Lysterium had become Liv's priority. Although Larry didn't know the real reason she'd left, he'd not taken her departure well. Liv was like a daughter to him, but if Liv had told him the truth, he would have thought she was crazy.

A month had passed since Liv had received Umaro's letter stating that she knew the whereabouts of Liv's father. Like all things traumatic, the letter had put Liv in a singular frame of mind. It was meant to taunt her, and it had succeeded brilliantly. Liv's single minded determination for answers brought a callousness toward all other things in her path. Little did she know, she had set herself on a path that would consume her, leaving behind a wake of destruction.

Wes, being Lysterian born and Liv's one true love, could see the changes, and through his vast otherworldly wisdom, he knew the progression of this madness. Wes was not only highly intelligent and powerful, but also the nephew of Umaro. He knew how her mind worked, and he knew her games and how she would use them to torment Liv until she had what she wanted. His knowledge of this made him nervous. What did Umaro want other than the obvious—to kill Liv? The real question was, what did she know that they didn't?

Until recently, Wes and Liv had only ever disagreed on matters of her safety, but this was different. Lately, all they did was fight. Liv had taken to pacing incessantly, and Wes's stylish pompadour was in a constant state of disarray from being ruffled by his hands. He had asked Amara, his mother, to come to Earth to discuss options, and she was on her way. Mainly, he wanted a ruling against Liv's irrational desire to plunge into the unknown and seek out Umaro. The tension between them had been building; this particular afternoon, both were approaching their boiling points.

Wes was exasperated. His platinum hair was sticking straight up; his eyes were wide. "Can't you see this is a trap? Clearly she is in control of the situation! She wants to kill you, and she will go to any length to see it done! Who knows what else she wants with you? Humans and your rash emotions, with no thought to consequences!"

Liv resumed pacing, threw her hands up and snarled, "Consequences be damned! I already know what needs to be done. I have to see her. I have to know!" She let out a growl of frustration. "So much time has already passed. I should have gone right away!"

Wes's voice was becoming angrier. "Are you even listening to yourself? You sound like a child!" He closed his eyes for a minute and calmed down. He walked over to Liv and put his hands gently on her face. He felt heavy with his many burdens, and spoke softly, "I don't want to fight with you. We've been through so much with Umaro. The Harbor is dangerous. This isn't like any danger on Earth; there are worse things to fear there, like madness."

Liv closed her eyes, pressing her rosy cheek into his hand. She looked up at him with pleading. "I have to know, Wes. Maybe I am acting like a child, but that's just it. I've never known my dad. What if she really does know where he is? My mom never told me anything about him. If he's alive and Umaro does know where he is, well, he is the only family member I have left. I deserve some answers from him."

Wes feared he was fighting a losing battle, something he was unaccustomed to. He didn't like it. Unfortunately, Liv was stubborn, and she knew what she wanted.

Amara's airy voice came from the doorway. "I believe I have arrived just in time."

The friction was still heavy in the room. Liv jumped and turned. "Thank you for coming, but I think it was a waste of your time." She walked over to Amara and handed her the letter.

As Amara studied the letter, Liv began to pace again. Wes was anxious for his mother's response.

"It's never a waste of time to visit my son and his lovely wife. I have to agree with Weston. It looks like a lure to me." She handed the letter back to Liv. "I know my sister. She's capable of unimaginable deceit and evil."

Wes could see that saying those words deeply hurt Amara. No matter what Umaro had done, they were still sisters, and they'd once been close.

Amara shook her head slightly and returned to the matter at hand. "She clearly has a motive for this, and whatever that motive is, it isn't good."

Liv stopped in midstride. "Look, I know how this appears to both of you. If I were in your shoes, I would probably be saying the same thing. But I know—or, rather, I feel—Umaro is telling the truth. I think she really does know where he is. I agree she probably has ulterior motives; nonetheless, I have to go. There's nothing more to discuss." She turned to Wes with a glare as she finished her statement.

Wes, frustrated, started to speak, but Amara touched his shoulder and said, "I think that before anything is done, we need to get the Book of Prophecy. It might have some answers on this matter if it concerns Liv. Most importantly, you should have a plan, and as of now you are grasping in the dark."

Liv's color drained. She hadn't been able to go to Mona's house since the murder. She spoke in a suddenly meek voice. "The Book of Prophecy?"

Wes gave his mother a worried glance knowing what she was asking of Liv.

Amara spoke gently. "I'm sorry, dear one. I know it must be difficult for you. I think it is necessary to seek guidance from the book."

Liv grimaced.

All Lysterian's are born with some form of power. However, the royal bloodlines were born with special abilities specific to their regions and needs, in order to rule, this power was called the Nomilis. Humans sometimes caught glimpses of the Nomilis, which was interpreted as "pyrokenesis", "telepathy", and so on, being only a legend or rumor on earth. Since Wes was a royal, his Nomilis included many important abilities to rule Elderwood. A surprising addition awakened in Wes when he fell in love with Liv, a form of empathy, which allowed him to radiate comforting feelings. He used that Nomilis on Liv now. "You can't hide from the house forever, love."

Liv closed her eyes. Wes could see she was allowing the Nomilis to wash over her.

"Okay," she said. "But I need to go alone. I can't handle other people there right now."

Amara looked concerned. "To my knowledge, Mona fought to prevent the chest being opened, which is why she was murdered. I don't think they retrieved her key. In the chaos, none of the Epoch had the book. I am hopeful it's still safe."

Liv raised her eyebrows. "None of us even checked after. I hadn't even thought of that until now! I couldn't go in there after—"

Swiftly, Wes used his Nomilis on her again, and he could tell she was grateful for the sense of calm relief it gave her. "I should go with you. There's still a chance of an attack. Nothing is safe right now."

"Wes, I just think I need some time to be alone. It's been a few months since the funeral, a month since the letter, and nothing's happened. I'll go to the police station and see if they have my grandma's key. She never took it off, so it should be in evidence."

He was about to protest, but he saw Liv's face fall. Since the blood oath had traded their places in Umaro's castle, Wes had had an even stronger connection to Liv, and he could hear her surface thoughts. He felt her emotions. She couldn't face what she needed to with anyone there; the pain that waited for her in the house filled with nostalgic torment was something that could not involve other people. It was too agonizing. The burden wasn't about the book or the pending decision of Umaro's letter; it was finally facing the fact that Mona was dead. Liv had made herself believe that if she avoided the home she knew and loved, maybe the loss wouldn't hurt as much. As soon as she entered, the situation would irrevocably become real, and she would no longer be able to question if Mona's death had been a dream.

He reluctantly acquiesced. "I won't be far. If anything happens, I will know, and I'll be there in seconds." He added with a hint of apprehension, "But I still think I should be with you,"

Liv gave him a halfhearted smile.

Amara looked at Liv with sympathy. "I will go back to Lysterium and see what I can find out. If Umaro is up to something involving your father, my cousin Olan should know. You saw him briefly in Umaro's castle, he rules Pyxis, which is where the prison and the Harbor are. If there's anything to find of her scheming, he will root it out. Let me know what the book shows you." She nodded to Wes as she left.

CHAPTER 2
Mona's Letter

THE FEW TIMES LIV MANAGED to drift to sleep that night, she had violent nightmares of Mona's death. Liv jolted awake at the image of her body draped over the chest in the library with unblinking eyes. The last image of her beloved grandmother was forever soiled. That morning, she found a note from Wes on his pillow. It explained that he had doubled the barrier spells around Mona's house and would be close by, waiting. Liv loved Wes, but she was relieved he wasn't home that morning. Her task was going to be arduous enough without him hovering over her.

She got out of bed and headed for the bathroom to brush her teeth and shower. She stared in the vanity mirror, examining the dark circles under her eyes. The weight of what she had to confront was incomprehensible. When she'd finished drying her long black waves, she pinned her hair in a side ponytail and put on a wool knit hat. Then she applied heavy liquid liner, mascara, and lip gloss. She threw on a pair of dark fitted jeans, wool boots, and a vintage herringbone sweater accented with a thin black belt at the waist. She headed downstairs to make some coffee. To her surprise, Wes had set a cranberry muffin on a plate, and steaming coffee was in her favorite mug with a second note beside it. Liv smiled. The cold day seemed warm from Wes's unfailing love for her.

My Darling,

If you decide you need me, I will come right over. I know you can do this.

I love you.

W.

Icarus, her Lysterian cat, jumped onto the counter to greet her with loud purrs. He always cheered her up, and she couldn't help but feel better when staring into his large jade eyes. Especially since finding out that he could talk when in Lysterium, and he knew everything that was going on long before she did. It was still a little strange for her. He was wise, kind, and like a son to her since she had raised him from kittenhood. Looking at his adorable face, with his long whiskers twitching slightly, she knew he understood everything, and it brought her comfort. She ran her fingers through his silky fur, rubbed his gray ears, and then gave him a kiss on the side of his twitchy whiskers with a bright smile.

Liv took a bite of the muffin and a swig of coffee, grabbed her coat and scarf from the rack by the door, and headed out, waving to Icarus as she shut the door. She decided to walk to the police station instead of taking a cab to give herself some time to prepare. She walked slowly in silent thought, trying to shut out the anxiety she was feeling. It was the middle of March and unseasonably cold, it penetrated her to the core, making it painful to breathe. She pulled her scarf up over her nose and mouth to stave off the ache in her lungs and tucked her hands into the deep pockets of her fitted wool coat.

The park, dusted with snow, looked enchanting. Icicles hung from the twisted, leafless branches. The metal of the benches was barely visible, all piled in white. It seemed the stark garden paths were right out of a black-and-white photograph. The winter smell in the air mixing with the warm exhaust from traffic and the various vendors on the sidewalks reinforced Liv's love of the city. Steam was rising from the local bakery, and bits of snow fluttered down from high in the sky but never seemed to make it far enough to reach the harried street.

It happened that today was Tuesday, which meant the police station would be slow. There wasn't much of a wait to speak with one of the officers who had worked on her case. Detective Connors walked through the waiting room toward Liv. He was a rugged, run-down type in his early forties, but he had a boyish charm behind his tired eyes and the streaks of gray in his hair. He recently had been promoted to detective, and he wore it well. He was single and had hinted that he found Liv to be exceptionally appealing. He took any opportunity he could to see her, although he usually became flustered when he was around her.

He cleared his throat nervously. "H-hello, Miss Worthington."

Liv smiled. "Please, Detective, I've asked you to call me Liv."

"Right. Mis-- uh—sorry. Liv, what can I do for you?"

Liv tried to focus on the business side of what she needed to ask. She didn't want to cry. She steadied her voice to a professional tone. "Detective Connors, I wondered if I could have a particular necklace that my grandmother always wore, back from evidence."

Detective Connors was noticeably upset. "I'm sorry, Miss Worthington, but evidence is held at a different station. You would need to go there to see the evidence log. If a case is still open, they usually won't release it. I'm sorry."

Liv's face fell. "Is there anything that can be done? It's just that it's a family heirloom, and my grandmother was the last living family I had. She raised me. It would mean so much if I could have it back."

Detective Connors shifted his weight, his forehead glistening slightly with sweat. "I can call over. If it's been processed. Maybe. I--I can try."

Liv gave him a red-carpet smile. "Thank you so much. That would be great."

Detective Connors seemed to relax a little. "Okay, I'll be back shortly."

He was gone for about fifteen minutes. Liv sat in the waiting room, watching people come in and out for small issues, such as photo radar tickets, complaints, and vehicles that had been towed. She couldn't help but feel as if all of that was meaningless. If the world really knew what was going on, would people care about a ticket?

She was lost in thought, when the click of the door opening brought her back, and Detective Connors walked toward her. He smiled. "You're in luck. The necklace was already processed by the crime-scene unit; it didn't contain any evidence pertinent to the case. I had to pull a few strings, but they will release it to you."

Liv stood and shook his hand with a genuine smile. "Thank you, Detective. I really owe you one!"

He blushed. "How's about we go for drinks?"

Liv held up her left hand, flashing the massive pink diamond. "I'm married, remember? Friends?"

"Right. The freakishly tall blonde guy. Uh—friends, of course. Glad I could help anyway."

Liv giggled as she pulled out a piece of paper and a pen from her bag. "Can I get the address, please?"

He gave her the information, and after Liv thanked him again, she left the building.

As it was, Liv knew the police were never going to find the person who'd murdered Mona, since he or she was in Lysterium. They'd marked the case as unsolved. Wes, who was experienced in deception and hiding the truth from humans since being sent to guard Liv on Earth, had offered to alter their perception on the case. He had wanted to avoid Liv going through more pain if the case was ever reopened, but Liv had declined. That was the least of her worries now.

The evidence station was on the other side of town, so Liv decided that taking a cab would be wise in the cold. To her delight, when she arrived at the station, she was helped right away. Detective Connors had done an exceptional job. She was able to get the necklace released quickly with a few signatures, and she was on her way again. Her shoulders relaxed slightly now that she knew the necklace hadn't been stolen, which meant the chest was still intact. She inhaled deeply, feeling comfort in knowing that the necklace Mona had always worn religiously was safe in her possession. Thinking of Mona, she looped the chain around her fingers absently as the cab drove, the cold metal warming against her skin. Liv paid the cabbie as they pulled up to the extravagant mansion. "Thank you!" she called as he pulled away.

She walked up the long driveway and climbed the porch steps slowly. She approached Mona's front door, reaching for her set of keys. Her stomach was tied in knots. On some level, she expected her grandmother to answer the door with her big southern greeting and her ten o'clock scotch. Her heart dropped as she realized that would never happen again. She stood at the front door, staring for what seemed like twenty minutes before actually unlocking it. She hesitated, turned from the door, and walked along the wrap-around porch, gently grazing her fingers along the railing, which had a fresh coat of snow. She touched the chain on the old porch swing, which jingled and swayed, and the dead leaves of the roses that climbed up the porch rails crunched under her feet.

She walked back down the steps, and her boots sank in the snow as she slowly tread the path toward the orchards. She stopped at the garden with many memories dancing in her mind. She felt that winter's icy suspension of life on the property, and the snow covering the house, were a tribute to her loss. It seemed the world missed Mona as much as Liv did and was grieving in its lasting cold. The wind suddenly picked up and dusted Liv's black hair with fine powder as it began to snow. The sullen quiet of the snow falling and the delicate wind grazing her face were both comforting and melancholy. The long stretch of orchard she had loved to get lost in as a child was almost haunting in the winter. Those times felt far away now. The ice-covered branches sparkled in the overcast light. The once well-maintained rows were now filled with rotten fruit, dead leaves, and overgrown with grass—a metaphor for the life that had been taken.

The chill, like her heart, was starting to throb, so she headed back up the path toward the house. She reached the steps and stopped again at the door; every time she thought of going in, flashes of blood and Mona's staring, unblinking eyes stopped her. She could feel the horrible grip of the Epoch holding her captive. That powerful seduction spell which couldn't be fought or broken until the Epoch chose to, was forced upon her multiple times both on earth and in Lysterium. She hadn't been there when Mona was murdered, unable to do anything as her world shattered. She shook her head as if to rid herself of the memories. She took a deep breath and finally turned the knob.

The heavy door creaked open, and white light flooded the rich entryway. Dust had gathered on the side table where Mona used to place her scotch. Dead flowers were in a vase of murky water, shedding petals at the foot of the umbrella stand and coat rack. It was too quiet; the air was musty from the house being empty. Wes had hired someone to clean up the biologicals, but there were boot prints all over the floor and remnants of fingerprint powder on the doorknobs and windows from the crime-scene specialists. As she shut the front door, the house became dark, lit only by shafts of gray light from the vast curtained windows. The place felt abandoned; it was eerily shadowed, silent, and dusty. These were not adjectives Liv would have ever used to describe Mona's house—her house, *their* house. But there it was, haunted and alone, suspended in time, devoid of all the light and joy that used to reside within.

Liv slowly walked toward the library. A soft thud and an echo announced each step of her boots. The sound of her heartbeat throbbed in her ears. She didn't make it in, but stopped at the doorway, surveying the room. Although the blood was gone, the room still resembled a crime scene. The furniture had been shuffled in the struggle, and it didn't look like the room she knew so well.

Liv kept walking past the library, up the rich mahogany spiral stairs, leaving a faint trail with her fingertips in the dust on the banister. She reached Mona's bedroom, which was feminine and warm, filled with gaudy details that were Mona in essence. She stood at the door, taking in everything.

The ostentatious sleigh bed had a large tufted fabric head and footboard that were the height of luxury. The old stone fireplace, which had a huge sheepskin rug and chaise lounge in front of it, was black with use. Dozens of black-and-white photographs covered the mantel. The fireplace was flanked with built-in bookcases that held volumes of photo albums labeled by year, old diaries and journals, antique first-edition books, and old scrapbooks filled with newspaper clippings.

Adjacent to the bed was an exquisite vanity that looked as if it belonged in Marie Antoinette's dressing room. It was filled with makeup. A Victorian brush and mirror on a silver platter rested on the corner of the table with old atomizer perfume bottles. Necklaces and hats hung from the corners of the gilded mirror. A beautiful jewelry box was in the center. Near the jewelry box was the last picture Liv had taken with Mona, framed. They'd taken it just that fall, before she knew about Lysterium—before everything changed. They were sitting on the porch swing with their feet up, laughing. Larry, Liv's boss, had taken the candid when he dropped off some edits for her over the weekend on his way out of town. He had framed it for both of them; it was one of Liv's favorite pictures. She touched the picture, and tears swelled. She remembered that day well; she could hear Mona's laughter resonating throughout her memory. After seeing all the treasured recollections, Liv was grateful she had an eternal part of Mona with her. She remembered all the good times she'd had in the house and all the love that had filled it for decades.

She saw that Mona's ostrich-feather robe was laid out near the foot of the bed. She picked up the robe, bunched it up, and buried her face in the fabric. She took a deep breath. The smell of lilac and Yves Saint Laurent still lingered, and she found herself weeping into it. The scent of her grandmother provided one last consolation for her aching heart.

After a long time, Liv laid the robe back on the foot of the bed and smoothed it out so it looked perfect. She walked over to the mantel, and her fingers caressed the frames delicately as she soaked in all the pictures she had loved to look at as a child—Mona's fondest memories. Pictures of her wedding day and youth, her parents, and old friends were joined by cute candids with her husband, Kinsey, as they grew older. There were also pictures of Liv's mother, Evelyn, as a child; old family pictures taken in Louisiana when Mona was a child; photos of various ages of Liv; and many of Kinsey, Mona, Evelyn, and Liv together.

As she passed the vanity to leave the room, she stopped when she noticed an envelope with her name on it. Her brow rose. "What?" she said aloud, picking up the envelope. She opened it to find a copy of Mona's will, a letter, and some old photographs. The letter was dated the day of Mona's murder.

Dear Sugar Pea,

Your involvement in this mess was not what I wanted for you. I tried to keep you out of it, but it seems you were meant to play a role in this story for reasons I don't yet know. Things are getting more dangerous for all of us. As you are my only heir, I have enclosed my will in case anything should happen, but most importantly, I thought you should know the truth. Your mama never wanted me to tell you about your father; she made me promise, but I've held on to this long enough. Honestly, I don't know much. She kept a lot of information from me. I found these pictures in one of her journals after she died. I thought you should have them.

His name was Lucian. Evelyn called him Luc. He was a sea captain. They met when he came to port in the city for a few days. Though they only dated for a month, your mama was head over heels in love with him. He claimed to have loved her and even stayed longer than he should have to be with her. When he left, he promised to write to her every day and come back as soon as he could. Shortly after his departure, she found out she was pregnant, and she wrote him a letter to tell him the news. She told him she wanted to get married, but she never heard from him again. She was, of course, devastated, and she never wanted you to know how he broke her heart. I don't know his last name, where he was from, or how you could ever contact him, but now you know the story.

I spoke with Amara. I know I was being unfair about Wes. He's a good man. I know that. I just wanted you to have some kind of normal life. I suppose that wasn't destined for you. I want to give you my blessing. I know he will take care of you; he has loved you for a very long time. He must have asked me a dozen times for my blessing, and I would never give it to him. It seems you two were meant to be together one way or another.

I have left everything to you. It is my greatest wish that you take over the house and have children who can grow up here and share all the history and memories we have spent a lifetime building in it. I hope I can be there to see your children and watch your life blossom into new seasons. If I am not, and you are reading this, know that I am so proud of the woman you have become, and I will always live in your heart. I love you more than you could ever know, Sugar Pea, and I always will.

Grandma

Liv stared at the letter, she read it twice, as tears splattered onto the page making the paper slightly translucent in spots. She held it tight to her chest. It was as if Mona had known she was about to meet her death. Liv felt lost, but the letter meant so much to her. She got to hear Mona's voice one last time and have a letter with her love in it. Finally, she let go and began to sob loudly. Her whole body shook. Despite going through so much tragedy, she hadn't let herself truly grieve. She lay on the bed for a time, holding the letter and staring at the window while she cried. When she had calmed down, she sat up, wiped her face and neck, and smoothed her hair back under her hat.

Liv pulled out the photos. The first was of Evelyn and a man with his arm around her waist. She was looking up at him, and they both had radiant smiles. Evelyn wore a tea-length floral dress with a fitted bodice. Her black curls blew against her neck and chin in the wind, and her dress blew against one side of her body. They stood on a shipping dock, and the background included an overcast sky, a large ship, and the rippling sea. The picture was old, black and white, and worn by years. Small wrinkles creased the edges, marks from being handled. Her mother couldn't have been more than twenty in the picture, and she was lovely. The couple looked happy. Liv had never seen her mother look at anyone so adoringly. She really had been in love. Liv flipped the picture over. "Me and Luc" was written in her mother's handwriting. She flipped it back over and touched her mother's face in the picture. She felt an ache in her heart, missing her and her bright smile, which could light up a room.

She picked up the other picture, which was in faded color. It was Lucian from the waist up, standing on a ship. Seeing a close-up picture, Liv realized how striking their resemblance was. She had the beauty of Evelyn and Mona, but every feature proved she was his. He was young and exceedingly handsome. His coarse, wavy brown hair was slicked back with a gel, which accentuated his large green eyes—Liv's eyes. His face was perfectly proportioned and masculine, with a dashing smile and tan skin. He was well built, with strong arms and rough hands. In the picture, he was laughing and holding the helm of a ship. His clothes were simple and slightly dingy: a white fitted T-shirt, jeans, and a belt. He had a pack of cigarettes rolled up in his sleeve and a captain's hat under his arm. Liv flipped the picture over: "My Luc and his ship."

Liv placed the letter and pictures back in the envelope and tucked it safely in the inside pocket of her jacket. Her face flushed. How could he have abandoned them? They looked so happy. She didn't understand and wanted answers more than ever.

After spending a long time in Mona's bedroom, Liv felt it was time to face her fear and go into the library to get the Book of Prophecy. She studied the rooms below as she slowly made her way down the spiral staircase. She took in the opulence of the old Victorian home and all of its charm. Her hands trembled as she walked to the room that once had been her favorite in the house. When she reached the mahogany doors, she focused on emptying her mind, pushing all thoughts away. There it was: the chest. The last time she had seen it Mona was dead. She walked to the chest, shut her eyes tightly, pulled out the key, and knelt. She could see that Mona's blood had seeped into the cracks of the wood. Salty tears fell onto the chest, turning watercolor red as they made contact with the old blood. She traced the wood grain with her fingers and traced the monogrammed *M*. She thought of how many times she had begged Mona to reveal the secret of this chest and how, ironically, this chest was the object that had caused her so much pain in the end. She wished the chest had never been there. She wished she could turn back time and have Mona back, but she couldn't.

She put the key in and heard the lock click as she turned it. She opened the chest slowly, and as the lid creaked open, the smell of antiquity filled her nose. She stared blankly. The book was gone. "Oh God."

CHAPTER 3
Gone

Wes burst through the front door. "Liv?" He looked around for her.

Liv ran out of the library. "Wes?" She sprinted to him and grabbed his arm to pull him toward the library. She stopped suddenly. "How did you know?"

"I had a bad feeling. Ever since the blood oath"—he touched his chest—"I'm completely connected to you. I can sense when you're distressed."

Liv didn't understand how that worked, but she was too distracted to get the whole story. Anxiety peaked in her voice. "I don't know how it happened. Follow me."

They went into the library, and Liv opened the chest. "How could the book be gone? We got there right after—grandma—you called the police before we were taken prisoner. The police didn't open it; the key was in evidence, so they couldn't have. The chest is from Lysterium, so it's impenetrable without the key, right?"

Wes nodded anxiously.

The only items that resided in the chest were a compass and a map. Liv had seen both once before, when Mona showed her the Book of Prophecy. She picked up the compass and looked it over. There was an inscription on the back: "To my love, now I can be with you whenever you sail. Evelyn."

There was a small lip to the side. Liv opened it and discovered a picture of her mother inside the hidden chamber. She stared at the picture, perplexed. "This must have been my father's."

Wes stared at the chest for a long time. He could usually bring his Nomilis of magical comfort to Liv, but now he was creating the opposite effect with his silence. Liv was becoming increasingly more stressed the longer he stood there.

Liv's voice cracked. "What do we do? How did this happen?"

"I had hoped there was a chance the book was secure." His eyes were still searching the chest, as if he were waiting for something to appear. He looked pale and tense. Then something caught his eye on the floor near the chest. He hurried to pick it up, his face horrorstruck. It was a broken chain.

Liv went pale at his expression. "What is that? I've never seen it before. You're scaring me, Wes."

He held up the chain and slowly spoke. "This is the necklace I gave to Mona."

"You gave my grandma a necklace? For her pocket watch?"

He was still stunned. "No. It used to have the blood-oath vial on the end. When a blood oath is made, it contains the blood of the one making the oath and the one the oath is for. So both of our blood is in there. I think Umaro specifically went after the vial so that if she tried to kill you, I couldn't take your place. Only the Epoch wouldn't be able to destroy it, I used old magic, which is why I died."

Liv rubbed her forehead. "How did you get my blood?"

"Mona got some for me when you were fifteen, when I made the oath to her, just in case you ever had to go to Lysterium. You pricked your finger on the rosebush, and she cleaned it up. She saved it for that reason. The oath activated when you put on the pocket watch I gave you."

Liv remembered that day clearly. She felt strange that so much had gone on behind her back as a youth. She furrowed her brow. "Wait. If I have Grandma's key, then how did Umaro get the chest open?"

"She must have found one of the lost Iron Keys."

"Huh?"

Wes continued, "There were five keys made in the Iron City. They had an enchantment placed on them by the prophets; the keys were made to unlock anything, but only one could unlock the book. All of them were lost centuries ago during the wars. My parents spent the better part of a decade searching for the missing keys. They found three, including the key to the book, which my mother had and Umaro stole when she captured her. Mona had another, and my father has the third key. The other two are still unaccounted for."

Wes sat down heavily in one of the chairs by the fireplace. He slid his hands in his hair and rested his forehead in his palms. He sighed. "Umaro wouldn't have sent an Epoch to come get the book unless she had a guarantee of getting into the chest. I don't think Mona would have been killed over the book. I'm certain she fought over the book, but my mother would have told her to stop to spare her life. I think she died fighting over the blood-oath vial. The Epoch must have ripped it off of her after—"

Wes halted and immediately lowered his eyes, the crease in between his brows continued to his forehead. His words had knocked the wind out of Liv. Her face fell, turning red, and tears dripped down her cheeks.

Wes stood up and quickly embraced her, holding her to his chest. "I'm sorry. I wasn't thinking. I didn't mean to say that so tactlessly."

"It's not that. It's just that if she hadn't fought him, she would still be alive. Why didn't she just let him take it?" she wailed. "She knew she was no match for an Epoch! She died protecting me. She died over the stupid blood oath!"

Her tears quickly turned hot with anger. Why had Mona been so careless with her own life? Why couldn't she have just let him take it? She screwed her face up. "And there's this." She pulled out the envelope from her coat pocket and handed it to Wes.

He read it quickly and then looked at Liv with grief marring his handsome features.

She could feel the warm blanket of his Nomilis covering her again. "It's like she knew she was going to die, isn't it? Why would she write a letter like this that night? Right after we left! I don't understand what's happening."

Wes handed Liv the letter back and went to hug her, but she stepped away and started pacing.

"What does this mean? Umaro has the book, so that means she will have a weapon. What if she escapes? What if she had a plan when she was captured and taken to the prison beyond the Harbor? She didn't put up much of a fight when they took her."

"Liv, stop. You're going to give yourself an aneurysm. There are a lot of questions that need answers, but I don't have them. I need to meet with Olan to find out if he has any information. I should leave tonight. I'm not sure when I'll be back, but I will let you know anything I find out."

She stopped pacing and gave Wes a glare that could have singed his eyebrows off. "I'm not staying here to wait! I'm going with you. I planned to go all along, ever since the letter arrived. There is no way you're leaving me here and going off to find out all the answers of my life!"

Irritation crept into Wes's voice. "Liv, Umaro has the blood-oath vial. She will break the blood oath! She could curse you with this. Or worse, she could control you if she knows how to use it properly. Don't you see? You are completely unprotected and vulnerable right now."

This revelation halted Liv's fury for a moment. Honestly, she was slightly relieved that Wes could no longer bear the burden of her affliction She had almost lost him because of that blood oath. She kept this thought to herself. She was, however, worried about what Umaro could do to her now that she had the vial. "Then how do we stop her from doing those things to me?"

Wes rubbed his eyes with his first finger and thumb. "If she destroyed the vial, then the oath will be broken. But if she altered it, who knows what she could accomplish? I have to speak with Eljene about it. This changes everything."

"Then let's go! Right now, I'm ready."

Wes looked unnerved. "Liv, you are not going! It's too dangerous. We don't know what to expect at this point."

She let out a screech of anger and stormed past him, too enraged to talk anymore.

"Liv, where are you going?" Wes called after her.

"For a walk!" she yelled, slamming the door.

Liv walked through the park; it was the longer route back to her apartment. She needed to calm down. The snow was falling more heavily, the sky was gray, and the icy wind hindered visibility. It was quiet; the park was empty. The concise sound of the snow crunching under her boots with each step, the wind howling through the naked trees, and a crow cackling personified the loneliness she felt. She folded her arms against the cold. New York was her home, and it always had the ability to slow her thoughts, quiet her soul, and soothe her. When she was halfway to her apartment, she realized how unreasonable she had been. *He was only trying to protect me*, she thought. Shame filled her. She had gravely overreacted. Going into the house and viewing all the things that reminded her she would never see Mona again had caused her emotions to be unstable. She hoped Wes would forgive her irrational behavior. She took her time, feeling a nervous knot in her stomach about having to face him. It seemed they were always either in mortal peril or fighting lately.

When she reached the apartment, she slowly walked up the steps and opened the door. Wes was sitting on the couch with thoroughly ruffled hair and a scolded-puppy look on his face. She ran toward him. He quickly stood as she collided into him, holding him tightly. "I'm sorry. I just don't know how to deal with all of this."

"I hate fighting with you. I'm sorry. It's been my job to protect you for so long that I forget sometimes that now I'm a husband too." He held her face. "I love you. I just can't risk anything happening to you."

"Wes, I'm going to Lysterium. I don't want to fight anymore either. I can't stand it. I just need to change and pack a few things, and then we should go." Liv turned and walked up the stairs to the bedroom.

Wes was in the room before she was. "Liv, you can't go without the blood oath. Anything could happen. You could be killed! You have to stay here, where you will be safe."

Liv's voice was sharp with agitation again. She pulled her shirt off and glared at Wes. "Don't you think that Umaro could kill me here just as easily? At least I have a fighting chance in Lysterium with you and your family." She dug through her dresser. "Remember what happened to my mother. Umaro broke into a portal and came to Earth, and it was here she murdered my mother. It's not like she couldn't find a way to get to me if she was really determined. And I still have an elemental stone, it did its job and unlocked powers in me, I can fight, Eljene can still make a lifesaving elixir from it. Plus my tears—" Liv threw on a camisole and then grabbed a pink cardigan with pinwheels sewn to the shoulders and started buttoning it. "We can figure this out together in Lysterium. This is the best option. I'm going with you."

Wes had never looked anything less than handsome. He was *GQ* worthy and more; however, the weight of this horrible situation had left him looking a bit worse for wear. He made a frustrated sound and violently rubbed his hands through his bright hair, causing it to stick up in all different directions. "I can't win here!", he bellowed.

Liv, who was slipping on a pair of shoes, stopped midway, taken aback. He had never yelled like that. Wes was always composed and gentlemanly. "Wes, I'm sorry you're mad at me."

Wes's anger ebbed. "I could never be angry with you. I'm angry at the circumstances. There are no good options here. We are, as you would say, between a rock and a hard place."

Liv was leaning against the dresser, as she finally slipped her other shoe on. Wes walked over, kissed her forehead, and then rested his chin on the top of her head. Liv breathed in his scent and closed her eyes, the simple pleasure of his contact calmed her.

He sighed. "I just don't know what to do. I can't lose you. Even with the elemental stone, you are so fragile. You are still human."

Liv moved her head back to look at him, stood on her toes, and took his face in her hands. "Listen to me. I know it's scary. But I know what I have to do, and running away from all of this is not it. I have to go with you, and I think you know that too. Whether you admit it or not, we're wasting time arguing."

Liv hadn't taken her pocket-watch necklace off since they'd come back to Earth. It was necessary to have a watch in order to travel from Lysterium to Earth because Lysterium time is much slower; if someone returned to earth without a watch time couldn't find them, and therefore could be lost forever. She tucked it into her shirt, placed Mona's envelope and the compass in her pocket, and grabbed a large tote. She walked into the bathroom and grabbed a toiletry bag she had ready for when she went out of town, and then she went back into the bedroom and put underwear, clothes, and a pair of shoes into the tote, along with the toiletry bag and a sweater. She slung the tote over her shoulder and headed downstairs, where Icarus stood by the door. He rubbed his head against her leg and meowed.

"You ready to go?" Liv said as he purred. She went to the coat rack. "One more thing." Before Icarus had time to protest, Liv shoved his head and arms into a little sweater. "It's cold out there." She smiled and said in a high-pitched voice, "You look so cute in your little kitty sweater." She put on her scarf and coat as Icarus glared up at Wes with his ears back. Wes chuckled under his breath and shrugged. When Liv was bundled up, she turned to Wes, slinging the tote over her shoulder. "Which portal are we going to take?"

Wes looked uneasy. "The one in the park, close to where you saw me for the first time."

Liv had a moment of nostalgia. So much had changed since then. As she opened the door, Wes snapped his fingers, and suddenly, he was wearing a gray peacoat and a black scarf, which made his pale features illuminate. Liv spread her arms toward Icarus, and the cat jumped up. She held him close to her chest, and the three of them headed to the park. They didn't speak. The ground was slick with ice, and puffs of smoke from their breath against the cold air floated up toward the sky. Icarus shivered slightly from the cold, and Liv held him tighter. They reached the same clearing where Wes had disappeared after they first met. It seemed as if it had been so long since that day. Up until that point, her biggest concern had been story deadlines, but all that was gone now.

Wes led them to an area thick with trees dusted with powdery snow. A few feet into the thicket, Wes stopped and bent down. He brushed his hand over a small stepping-stone covered with dead leaves and snow. "I will ask one more time for you to reconsider, Liv."

She looked at him for a long moment. He sighed and stepped onto the stone, holding his arm out for her. She stepped on and braced herself for the awful drop that was coming.

C HAPTER 4
Back to Lysterium

WHEN THEY ARRIVED AT THE crossroads, the carefree feeling of absent time and the unending desert of melted clocks were the same as Liv remembered. However, she had forgotten how frightful Argoth, the gatekeeper to Lysterium, was. When she saw him standing in front of the tree portals, her heart gave a jump, and she held Icarus tightly.

Icarus put a paw on her face. "It's all right, Mother. He's on our side."

Liv flinched. She still couldn't get used to her cat speaking. His voice was distinguished; she couldn't help but think of Sherlock Holmes when he spoke. She smiled at him. "Thanks, bud. He may be on our side, but he's still scary!"

Icarus let out a charming laugh.

Argoth's large wings, gray skin, and dozens of staring eyes were no less frightening than they'd been the first time she had seen him, and she was certain she would never get used to his imposing presence. Wes greeted him like an old friend, and they headed for the half circle of trees with the sign posts and turned toward the yellow tree that led to the Ashlands, where Eljene, Amara's cousin lived. Wes wanted to see her before they went on to speak with Olan, Eljene's brother, in Pyxis. They stepped onto the floating stone. The odd pulling sensation and the underwater feeling during travel made Liv feel disoriented.

The last time Liv had been in the Ashlands, she had traveled there escaping from the region of Torr, with Wes mortally wounded. It had seemed at the time dark and foreboding. Now the hues of the sand and horizon seemed brighter. The portal took them straight to the path under the canopy of yellow trees tenting the city. It was only a short walk to Eljene's.

Eljene waited outside, as if she had been expecting them. She stood with her arms folded against her dusty clothes and her multitiered monocle glasses nesting in her wild mess of bright orange curls, with pencils sticking out every which way. Resting in the long fingers of her right hand was a piece of parchment rolled up and tied with a string of leather.

As they approached, a large smile crept over her face. "I was wondering when you would arrive. Oh, Icarus, I didn't know you were coming!" Her high-pitched, airy voice was upbeat for the moment, and she scratched behind the cat's ears. "Well, hurry up!" She ushered them in the door. "There's going to be a storm tonight. Wouldn't want to get caught in it. I had to leave the dig site early. Pesky storms."

She was rambling on as usual, which was a comfort to Liv. She had always liked Eljene; of all the royals, with their elegant speech and high-class dress, Eljene seemed the most relatable. Liv set Icarus and the tote down and took her coat off. It was chilly in the Ashlands but nothing like New York.

Eljene walked out of the room, shouting behind her, "Anyone for tea?" Icarus trotted off behind her. She set down a bowl of chicken and then returned with three cups and an antique teapot, steaming from the spout.

Wes spoke as she poured. "Thank you, Eljene. We have some troublesome news."

Liv thought it was sort of funny how Wes always spoke to his family with an air of professionalism.

Eljene held up the parchment triumphantly. "Yes, yes. I received this from Pyxis not an hour ago."

Pyxis was the only water region in Lysterium. It was a vast shipping harbor worked by a network of sailors, merchants, and traders. Liv had only seen a few regions in Lysterium, and she was the most thrilled to see Pyxis.

Wes stared at the parchment with a baffled look. "What does it say?"

Eljene clapped her hands once loudly, causing Liv to spill a bit of burning-hot tea on her jeans. "Well, your mother received your message about the missing vial and told Olan to search Umaro's cell. No luck in that department. It wasn't there. So, he sent me a letter letting me know that you would be coming and that I needed to come up with a solution to help protect our little human here." She patted Liv on the top of her head and let out a piercing cackle.

Liv looked over at Wes, trying not to laugh. She cautiously relaxed. "So, then you aren't worried that she has the vial?"

Eljene stared at Liv for a moment. "Oh yes, dear, it's very worrisome. But there's not much we can do about it now. I made a potion for you to drink to help keep your mind and will in your control. Uma is a sneaky one, she is! I remember when we were children. She always found ways around the rules." Eljene stared off for a moment, apparently having a personal flashback. It was clear that Eljene couldn't let go of her love for her cousin, despite the darkness in her. Wes cleared his throat loudly, and she snapped back. "Right. As I was saying, Umaro will do whatever she can to harm Liv. But she doesn't have the full understanding of what she can do with the vial. That wisdom can only be possessed by someone of my position." She pointed at herself, beaming. "A brilliant chemist and potions master. They didn't assign me the Ashlands for nothing. I am one of four who can make an elemental stone. That's saying something!"

Wes's eyes rolled as Eljene went on her self-loving tangent. After a few minutes, she seemed to realize that she appeared a braggart and went back to the original subject. "My point is, I am qualified to place a temporary potion on Liv. Umaro will never be able to gain the full knowledge of the possibilities of a blood-oath vial. Her skills will be limited. But I'm quite certain she'll have mastered the mind-control aspect of it, which is why I have made this." She took a glass beaker off one of her four desks. It was filled with bright blue liquid, and gray smoke billowed out of the top.

Liv swallowed her sip of tea hard. "I have to drink that?"

Eljene held the beaker close to her face and inspected it, giving Liv a look as if to say, "What's the problem?" She shrugged. "I flavored it this time," she said with a hopeful tone.

Liv tentatively took the beaker. "So, what exactly will this do?"

Eljene took a sip of her tea. "Well, it blocks any outside forces that try to control you."

Liv's face lit up. "You mean the Epoch won't affect me while this is in my system?"

Eljene touched her nose, smiling as she swallowed another sip.

Liv looked at Wes as if he had just told her she won the lottery. "That's fantastic! I hate Epoch!"

Wes laughed genuinely for the first time in weeks.

Eljene interrupted. "I must warn you, though, dear, this potion does not work on the Sirens. So you will need to take precautions. Oh, and since your elemental stone enhanced your hearing, you will have to be extra careful."

Liv frowned. "The Sirens? Like the Greek mythology, Sirens?"

Since Eljene would have been labeled a genius on Earth, it was no surprise that she knew the planet's entire history. "Oh, they are much worse, my dear. Skilled hunters with terrifying beauty, and the luring enchantment they cast is unlike any curse you're likely to come across. Those old stories came from the sailors who traveled from Earth to Pyxis and had brief encounters with them. No, the Sirens are one of the deadliest forces in Lysterium. Can't be too careful. You will be passing right through their territory."

Liv felt her stomach drop. "We will?" She looked at Wes, her face showing clearly how disheartened she felt.

His tone was grim. "We'll have to pass through the Harbor of Lost Ships to get to the prison."

Liv had a thought and became hopeful. "Is there anything that can repel a Siren?"

Eljene spit her tea out as she burst into laughter. Liv was not amused. She wiped a spot of expectorated tea off her face and glared.

Eljene was still laughing. "My dear child, if there were, the Sirens would have been captured thousands of years ago. Oh, my word!" She laughed more. "And Pyxis would be free from their dangers. Of course there isn't anything that repels them."

Wes gave Eljene a stern look. Liv felt stupid for asking a question that was obviously naive.

Eljene, clueless of her insult, looked back at Wes. "What?"

Wes shook his head. "A little tact would be nice."

Eljene raised her eyebrows. "What? What did I say?"

Liv, realizing it was not Eljene's intention to ridicule, laughed it off. "It's fine." She had noted that most geniuses on Earth lacked certain social skills. Eljene was no exception to the rule. She was highly intelligent and odd, which, in Liv's opinion, made her more entertaining to be around.

Liv tried to sound upbeat and perky. "So"—she gave Eljene a sly look "what'd you flavor it with?"

"Vanilla cupcake!" She nodded proudly.

Liv held the potion up in a rather grim salute, remembering her last taste of Eljene's potions being too similar to fresh leaves. "Bottoms up." She drank the whole beaker in one continuous gulp.

The liquid did, in fact, taste like a vanilla cupcake—and, to Liv's surprise, it even had the texture of a cupcake. Liv licked her lips. "That's amazing! How did you get it to taste and feel like a cupcake?"

Eljene beamed. "Oh, that's nothing. How do you feel?"

Liv looked down at herself. "I feel fine. No change, really."

Eljene looked over. "Weston, if you will."

Liv looked over at Wes too. The space between her eyebrows crinkled. "What are you going to do?"

Wes gave her a look like that of a kid caught with his hand in the cookie jar. "Well, I have some small measure of telepathy manipulation Nomilis. Nothing like my mother's vast skill. I started exploring it after you said I could comfort you."

"Oh—Wait! Have you used this on me besides just comfort? And why am I just finding this out?" she huffed.

Wes laughed. "No. I promise. If I had, you wouldn't be in Lysterium right now."

"Good point" she relaxed.

Wes rubbed his hands through his hair and then focused on Liv. "All right, I'm going to put a thought in your head. Tell me if you feel persuaded to do it." A minute passed. "Anything?"

Liv shrugged and shook her head.

"Well, that's good, but I wish we had something stronger to test it on. Like an Epoch."

Liv's eyes widened. "I can cross that bridge when I come to it, pal."

Wes grinned. "All right, no Epochs." He put his hands up in surrender.

Wes walked over to Eljene, gave her a small hug, and headed for the door. "Thank you for making that ahead of time, Eljene. This will be very helpful. We should be going; we need to get to Pyxis. There's still a lot to do to prepare for the journey."

"No trouble. Watch out for the storm. It's going to be a nasty one." She slid her glasses on and walked out of the room, giving a small wave behind her.

Liv called Icarus, who ran out of the kitchen and followed them out the front door.

The vast desert always had a constant haze of ash. That day, the ash seemed to be light, like fresh snowfall flittering, and it gave the region a sense of enchantment. A soft breeze rippled the sand picking up fallen leaves in a swirl. The Jewel Mountains glistened in the red sunlight. Liv thought the land seemed to be more at peace with the fires of Torr since Umaro was no longer in control there. There were more of the spindly legged elephants carrying the many different creatures of Lysterium in the distance now, seemingly feeling more safe to be out in the open. The canopy of trees seemed more vibrant and full. Everything felt more secure. Liv was able to take in the full beauty of the Ashlands now that there was no longer a sense of danger lurking close by. She understood now why Eljene loved living in this region; it was full of mystery and charm. She noticed dark clouds working their way toward the city—the storm Eljene had spoken of.

Wes took Liv's hand as they walked to the edge of the cobblestone walkway. "As Pyxis is the next region over, I think flying would suit us just fine." He looked up at the sky. "It will take time for the storm to come in."

Liv looked out at the clouds. "Sounds like a plan."

Although Liv did not enjoy flying, due to the frightful speed and height, it was a beautiful day. Entering Pyxis from an aerial view would be dreamlike. Wes picked Icarus up with one arm and grabbed Liv by the waist with the other, holding her tightly. His body pressing against hers made her feel safe.. They quickly rose high into the air and began the fast journey to Pyxis.

Liv could see the Ashlands whipping by in a tan blur. Up ahead, she started to make out the glittering pale blue of the sea. She shouted against the wind, "Wes, slow down!"

She wanted to drink in every detail as they approached the long-awaited Pyxis. It was more than she could have imagined. The sea was like millions of diamonds sparkling, stretching infinitely in front of them. The water was a crisp, clear turquoise blue. There were few houses in Pyxis; ships were the predominant living arrangement. Each ship was unique and well crafted, highly decorated with copious details. The ships drifted in whimsical reverence, heightening the magic that seemed to encompass the city.

Near the entrance of the city Liv saw an immense golden statue of three women towering more than twenty stories tall. The statue showed women draped with fabrics; long, flowing hair; and winged ankles. They were standing, facing outwards, in a circle. The woman facing the dock was holding a ship's wheel, the woman on the right held a harp, and the woman on the left held a bird in her palm. The carvings were extremely lifelike, as if real giant women had been covered in melted gold.

Liv gasped with wonder and excitement.

Suddenly, Wes turned left and took them down slightly. "I'm taking us straight to Harp Isle, Olan's home. We need to meet up with him first. I will take you to see the city later."

Although she was disappointed, Liv nodded. She could see the city disappearing in the far distance as they flew in the opposite direction.

CHAPTER 5
Harp Isle

THE AIR WAS VIBRANT AND salty as they flew along the vast ocean. As Harp Isle came into view, Liv's mouth dropped open slightly. The island floated in midair. It stretched for a few miles horizontally, bordered by ever-flowing water cascading down the sides in a continuous waterfall to the sea far below. Wes set them down on a pathway that weaved through the high and low ground. There were tide pools scattered throughout, filled with crystal-blue water, mermaids, fish, and other strange creatures. On the higher plains was lush green vegetation. Hundreds of golden birds sang and frolicked in the air, wildflowers bloomed everywhere, and hefty shade trees were scattered all around.

On the farthest side of the island from where they stood was Olan's home, a massive Viking-esque ship made out of a combination of soapstone and wood. The architectural craftsmanship was exquisite. It floated in a deep pool of water with a winding stone staircase leading to the entrance. Curved black metal lampposts lined the staircase to the door on either side. Only about three feet tall, each had a large spiral that came out where the lamp was held. Below the spirals were metal birds, resembling a sand piper, holding vivid crystal lamps in their beaks. The lighting was soft and inviting against the setting sun, sultry water, and green gardens. Liv, Wes, and Icarus walked up the stairs and came to double doors carved with wings filling the entirety of the wood. On both sides of the doorway was a life-size statue of a woman draped in chiffon, with wings on the ankle, carved in alabaster.

Liv was overwhelmed. "I can't believe how amazing this place is. Just when I think Lysterium can't get any more surprising, you take me here!"

"I knew you would like it. We'll be traveling throughout Pyxis for quite a while. Although there are beautiful parts, we will be going to the darker parts soon enough. Then we'll see how you view Pyxis."

Liv couldn't imagine anything here bothering her. She didn't know what it was about the sea, but it always made her happy and calm, as if it would wash over her and carry away her worries with its soothing lullaby. She had been captivated by the ocean from birth, it seemed, and she couldn't explain why. Discovering that her father was a sailor had made her think that perhaps it was in her blood.

Now that she was in Pyxis, that feeling was constant. "I'm sure even the scary parts are beautiful. Look at Torr." She shrugged.

Wes straightened his shoulders, knocked three times and the door opened seemingly by itself. They made their way to the main room.

The grand ship was two stories. High ceilings and grey maple flooring, that was ashy and light in color, were the first things Liv noticed. The entryway's ceiling was about four feet taller than the rest of the ship, with a decadent chandelier reflecting a prism of light as it hung above their heads. To their left was a beautifully carved stairway and banister made of solid wood. Past the stairs was the main room of the house, which boasted an enormous alabaster fireplace. Lining the walls were impressionist-style paintings of water nymphs and mermaids, embraced lovers in flight, wonderful landscapes, and old chart style maps of the passages in Pyxis, and larger maps with all of Lysterium. Large dark pieces of furniture with luxurious fabrics rested on heavy rugs. The fireplace was the centerpiece of the room and was flanked on both walls with bookcases. Maps, journals, ancient-looking books, and other keepsakes filled the shelves. The room was masculine yet cozy and welcoming, with feminine touches

As they walked past the stairs and main room, deeper into the house, they turned right and entered an immense dining hall that held several old craftsman wooden tables. The largest was off to the left of the room and could have seated half of Pyxis, Liv thought. Antique wooden benches carved with wings on the ends sat at each table, and a row of metal chandeliers boasting dozens of candles hung above. This room was much more rustic than the other parts of the house and had a feel of warm invite and many gatherings.

Through the dining hall was an office, which was to be their final destination. The office, if one could call it that, was in fact more like a small house in size. The room opened up to a wall of windows that overlooked the city in the distance. Two large wooden desks with scrolled inlays and paintings of blue-and-yellow birds faced each other overlooking the view in the center of the room. A feminine, green high-backed chair was parked at one of the desks, and a tufted brown leather chair sat in front of the other. A cavernous fireplace was settled next to the wall of windows, burning low and crackling. The wall opposite the fireplace was entirely covered in apothecary drawers inset into the wall. As Wes and Liv entered the room, their hosts joined them.

Having only met Olan once, and under extreme circumstances, Liv felt embarrassed at seeing him again after her behavior with Umaro. The woman standing beside him, however, she had never seen before.

Wes smiled brightly. "Olan, thank you for seeing us."

Olan walked over and embraced Wes in an exuberant bear hug. He slapped Wes on the back when he was finished. "Good to see you in better health, my boy." His deep, burly voice offset his beaming face.

Liv's first impression of Olan had been that he was a strict, reserved man. Now that she was seeing him in his own home and in better circumstances, he was startlingly different. He was handsome but in a severe way. He was tall, with orange hair like Eljene, however his was mostly white with age, and his eyes were an unnatural blue. His frame was brawny, and he had calloused hands and heavy scarring on his arms and neck. He was friendly and warm. Liv knew he was a great ruler, and she had seen his disciplined and rather scary side, but he seemed to be laid back and hearty now.

She liked this side of him and was relieved when he approached her with a smile and said, "Considering the situation we were in the first time, we were never properly introduced. I'm Olan." He gave a slight nod toward his companion. "And this lovely creature is my wife, Coralis."

Her hourglass figure was accentuated by white vinyl leggings that hugged her frame as she moved closer to them. Her waist-length pastel teal curls bounced as she walked and were enhanced by the long sleeveless red tunic she was wearing. She wore her hair full and cascading down the sides of her face, with white diamond combs pinning back pieces here and there to emphasize her lilac-colored eyes, the top lids were lined thickly in black, and her long lashes reached almost to her perfect brow. Her ivory skin, with soft rose undertones, shimmered where the light caught it with an almost pearlescent glow, accentuating her high cheek bones and perfect nose. Perhaps the most amazing part about Coralis, were the enormous white feathered wings protruding out of her shoulder blades, resting against her body, and dragging on the ground behind her.

Liv thought "Lovely creature" was the understatement of the century as she gaped unapologetically. She was easily the most stunningly beautiful woman Liv had ever seen. From what she had gathered, all women in Lysterium were beyond exceptional in beauty, which made her wonder what Wes had ever seen in her. But Coralis had an exotic, almost celestial presence.

Coralis's full, red painted lips curved up, radiating joy at seeing her beloved nephew. She gave Wes a long hug, closing her eyes, and sweetly spoke. "It's been much too long, Weston. I have missed your company."

Liv stared, widely, and then, realizing she was gawking, gave Coralis a true southern smile. "It's such a pleasure to finally meet you both."

As she walked toward Liv, her hair draped off her shoulder in a sultry way. The teal stilettos she wore made her height even grander. Coralis, in looks, was the closest thing to an angel that Liv had ever come across. She extended her hand to Liv "The pleasure is ours." Coralis extended her hand.

Liv backpedaled and couldn't articulate anything comprehensive. Then she said in awe, "You're the most beautiful woman I've ever seen in my life."

Coralis laughed softly. "Well, thank you, dear. That's very kind of you." Her voice was like honey on a summer day, warm and rich. She was the epitome of elegance.

Olan winked at Liv and whispered, "She has that effect on humans." Then, in a booming voice, he said to everyone, "Well, shall we go to the main room and sit?" He started walking toward the door.

Liv looked up at Wes, mortified at her crudeness, and red faced. "Don't say it."

He chuckled.

Olan led them to the main room with the grand fireplace. Now that they were actually in the room, Liv could see it had an eighteenth-century feel to it. On the mantel were a model of an old-looking ship and a wooden box resembling a cigar box, with an old-fashioned metal lock. Multiple compasses, clocks, and candles dripping with wax filled up the rest of the mantel. Large

Victorian sconces were paired up on all the walls, giving the room a romantic cast of light along with the fire. She glanced around taking in the room.

When they were all comfortable, he and Wes broke into conversation. They were catching each other up on everything they knew.

Olan's tone was serious. "Nothing has changed at the prison. Umaro hasn't attempted anything. Although I wouldn't put it past her to have a macabre plan brewing."

"We need to head for the prison as soon as poss—"

Olan interrupted Wes, with a rapid-fire delivery, his mouth going off like a machine gun. "Of course, of course! I have already arranged for a ship and captain. He's a little crude and sometimes hard to understand." Liv made a confused face. "He's Irish. Human," Olan said, barely skipping a beat. "He's a bit crazy in the head. I suppose you'd have to be to want to sail through the Harbor all the time. But he's a phenomenal sailor, a good fighter, and as smart as a whip." Wes opened his mouth to say something, but again, Olan interrupted. "Oh—and he invented some great ear protection against the Sirens." Olan looked off in the distance and mumbled, "Sirens—terrible creatures always causing me grief."

Liv snickered to herself, she could tell Olan and Eljene were siblings. They had similar mannerisms and lack of social filters. Liv had heard stories about what a skilled sailor Olan was, and he was gifted with great intelligence, as Eljene was. It was interesting to see the similarities in them now that Olan was in his element.

Wes cleared his throat loudly. "You won't be sailing with us?"

Olan shook his head abruptly, appearing to have snapped out of his thought. "I'll accompany you, but I won't be the captain. Taking Umaro to the prison was enough for me for a while, since I retired years ago."

"You're the best sailor in Lysterium," Wes argued.

"Finn is more than qualified." He clapped Wes hard on the back. "Don't worry."

"I appreciate you setting that up. When can we meet him?"

"I've arranged for you to meet in the morning. He wants to stock up on supplies; I thought it would be a good chance for you to get to know each other. We'll set out for the prison in two days."

Coralis looked at Olan and said gently, "My darling, Weston and Liv are probably tired after all they've been through. Let's let them rest awhile."

Her voice seemed to melt away the long-winded tendency from Olan for the moment. "You're certainly right, my love. Where's my head?" He turned to Wes. "I'm happy to see you well, Westy! You had us real worried."

Coralis's stunning face fell into an expression of distress. "Yes, you did." She walked over and hugged him again. "I couldn't go through losing another one."

Wes smiled. "No need to worry. I'm perfectly fine now thanks to Liv and Eljene." He put his hand around Liv's waist, looking down to smile at her.

Liv blushed. "It was all Eljene." Then she furrowed her brow in a confused look, addressing Coralis. "What do you mean 'another one'?"

Coralis frowned, and shifted her weight while wrapping her arms around herself. She shook her head, and then looked at Liv with a cordial smile "A long story for another time, dear."

Olan stood and reached his arm out for Coralis who still seemed shaken. She snuggled up into his embrace as he spoke, "All right then, Orelia will show you to your room. We can discuss details after you've rested a bit."

Wes nodded to them as they exited the room.

A moment later, a small golden bird flew up to Liv. "It's an honor to meet you, Miss Olivia," the bird said in a high-pitched, silvery voice.

Liv let out a shriek and jumped back. "Jesus!"

The bird looked worried. "I'm terribly sorry, Miss Olivia. I didn't mean to frighten you. I'm Orelia."

Liv took a moment to restart her heart. "No, I'm so sorry." She felt stupid. "It takes some getting used to." Her cheeks flushed.

Orelia was sweet and cheery. "Not at all. Allow me to take you upstairs." She flew with fast-beating wings out of the great room.

Liv looked over at Wes with wide eyes, and he burst into laughter. She glared and rebutted in the snarkiest tone she could manage. "Oh, shut up, *Westy.*"

Wes's face fell into embarrassment. His tone was defensive. "He's called me that since I was born!"

Liv laughed as she walked toward the stairs. When they got to the room, it was just as extravagant as the rest of the house. Liv plopped down on the fluffy oversized bed and sighed. "It's crazy how much Olan is like Eljene." She was staring at the ceiling with one arm behind her head. "I love how quirky they both are." Wes walked over and sat down next to her. With her free arm, she pulled him down so he was lying next to her. "I'm so relieved he doesn't hate me."

Wes sat up immediately. "Why would he hate you?"

Liv blushed. She had forgotten that Wes had been technically dead when she'd lashed out at Umaro and Olan had intervened. "Well," she said, trying to find the right words, "when I first met Olan, let's just say he didn't have the best impression of me."

Wes furrowed his brow. "What do you mean?"

Liv sat up and leaned against her hand, looking at him. "That day—it was horrible. You were gone. I had to watch you die. After that, something in me snapped, and I went for Umaro while she was in his custody." Wes's eyes widened as she continued. "Olan was ready to attack me. Well, actually, he kind of did attack me. He used that magical telekinetic push Nomilis thing and slammed me to the ground to get me away from Umaro."

Wes stiffened and looked away. Liv put her hand on his. "You can't be angry with him; I was out of my mind. I was this screaming crazy person with a sword! Your dad stepped in before things got bad."

Wes didn't say anything.

"Wes?"

He stood up abruptly, his jaw clenched and body tense. "That's no reason to use that kind of brute force on any woman, especially a human!"

Liv stood up and turned his chin toward her gently. "Look, he did what he had to. It's over. Everything's fine now. I'm just relieved he was willing to look past all my crazy." She laughed, trying to lighten the mood. It didn't work. She raised one eyebrow. "Babe, it is what it is. Get over it."

Wes loosened a bit and smiled halfheartedly. "I don't remember anything that happened after I broke out of the coffin. I'm sure it was pretty bad, but he still didn't need to use that kind of force. You're human, and so fragile," he said as a final statement.

"So," Liv said, pulling her ponytail out and running her fingers through her messy hair, "what's the deal with Coralis? She's different from anyone I've seen in Lysterium."

Wes sat down and watched Liv comb through the knots in her hair, staring.

She looked around. "What? It's a mess. I know." She glanced in a mirror hanging beside the bed.

"I'm lucky," he said.

Liv looked down and smiled shyly. "Wes." She raised her eyebrows. "So? What is she?"

He lay back on the bed and put his hands behind his head. "She's half angel and half water nymph. She was born in Pyxis. She comes from a long line of royalty on the nymph side."

Liv's eyes lit up. "Wow, really? I knew there was something special about her. That's the most amazing thing I've heard! So, that's why she has wings?"

"Yes. Her father was an archangel, and her mother was a water nymph. She's unique, the only one of her kind. The water nymph's bloodline is extremely important to Lysterium. Pyxis was originally founded by the water nymphs, Coralis's ancestry. The nymphs had ruled Pyxis from the beginning, but then Olan was decreed the ruler and betrothed to Coralis. You know, my grandmother was a wood nymph."

"Really? You never told me that."

"Yeah, she was a pure-blooded wood nymph, and my grandfather was a pureblood royal descendant. Anyway, those were dark times, and Olan accepted his role and his arranged marriage gracefully."

"So, did they like each other at first?"

"Yes. Actually, the best part is that when Olan met Coralis, the tattoo ceremony happened instantaneously. They were both completely in love; it was a perfect match. So everyone was happy."

Liv beamed. "Wow. What a great happily ever after!"

Wes gave her a quizzical look. "Fairy tales?

Liv shook her head. "Never mind. Why is it that you know everything about me, and I hardly know anything about you?"

"What do you mean? You know me."

"I just mean the family history, like the nymph thing. I don't know anything about your past except what I've read in the Book of Prophecy."

Wes's face was weary from stress; his melancholy tone became apparent. "There's just so much history to tell. You forget I've been alive for thousands of years; it's not like a human lifetime. I promise that one of these days, we can have a full history lesson—when we aren't trying to keep from being killed."

Liv touched the tattoo on her chest and smiled. "I can tell they're still in love."

Wes stared absently as he spoke. "I've told you before that when someone of my bloodline is born, he or she is given certain items. Remember?" Liv nodded. "I'm told that when Olan was born, he was given a harp. Coralis's ancestors on her mother's side created Pyxis. The harp is the symbol for the city. Naturally, when he met Coralis, he was drawn to her beauty, but his feelings went much deeper than that. They are perfect for each other in every way. They married very young and have been happy ever since."

"What a great story. So, she's *really* half angel?"

Wes laughed. "Yes."

"I didn't even think that was possible." Liv felt exhilarated that she had met an actual angel. "I really wish I knew more about the history of Lysterium." She took the letter out of her jacket pocket and pulled out the pictures. She studied the photo of her father. "I wish I knew more about my *own* history." Her voice saddened.

Wes sat up and put his hand over the picture. "Maybe some things are better left unknown."

"Maybe you're right, but I still *have* to know. Do you think I will ever find him?"

"Let's not focus on that right now." Wes took the picture from her slender fingers and set it on the nightstand. "Tomorrow we'll meet Finn and see the city, and then we'll be heading out on a dangerous trip. Tonight, let's just not think about all that."

He kissed her shoulder, then slowly moved to her collarbone and up to her neck. She slid her hands under his shirt, moving them up his strong back, and eased off his shirt. Her eyes stopped at the long, thick scar across his chest, over his heart, and her face fell. It was a reminder of the blood oath Wes had made with Mona to replace Liv's death with his. The scar was brutal and still a dark pink, with ragged edges where the great sword had torn his flesh. Wes had died that day in Umaro's castle, and if it hadn't been for Liv's tears, he wouldn't have been there with her now.

She traced her fingers across the scar. "A constant reminder that I almost lost you." She rested her palm on the scar, covering his heart.

Wes put his hand on hers. "My heart is still beating. You feel it." He looked down tenderly at her. "I'm alive because of you. And I plan to be here for a long time." He smiled.

Liv was still frowning. "You wouldn't even have this scar if it wasn't for me."

Wes lifted her chin up toward him. "I wouldn't have it any other way. In that moment, I was happy to die for you, and I would do it again. I love you, and laying my life down for you is little sacrifice for your survival."

Liv felt a prick of fear. "Don't get any ideas, I couldn't bear it. It almost killed me when you died. I still have nightmares about it."

Wes kissed her, "I'm right here. You don't need to worry. Get some rest." She turned off the light.

Liv jolted awake to the sound of thunder crashing loudly. Wes wasn't in the bed, or even in the room; Icarus was asleep next to her. She quietly got up, went to the bathroom to brush her teeth, and then buttoned her long coat over her camisole and underwear. There was a small terrace to the side of the room; she opened the door, walked out onto it, and leaned against the railing. The storm had hit with a vengeance. The sky was black, heavy rain flooded overhead, streaming off the roof in sheets and lightning pierced the dark every few moments. She shivered against the wind and stared out at the choppy sea, lost in thought. There was nothing quite like a good storm, especially one over the ocean. She felt a presence behind her and turned.

Wes was leaning against the open terrace door with his arms folded. "Are you all right?"

She smiled rubbing her eyes. "Yeah, just thinking." She walked over to him, and they went inside. "How long was I asleep?"

Wes glanced at his pocket watch. "About six hours."

She took her coat off, stretching her arms as she did. "Wes, if the passage to the prison is so dangerous, why hasn't anyone come up with an easier route?"

He sat on the edge of the bed. "There used to be a safer transport; we created it during the wars. Eljene and Umaro came up with it. They were called vanishing stones. After Umaro turned on us, they were outlawed. They were too dangerous to use, because Umaro had aided in the invention. The risk she'd use them to break prisoners out was too great. So they were ordered to be destroyed, although I'm sure a few are still out there."

"What's to stop her from making a new stone and breaking herself out?"

"Umaro can't make new stones without Eljene. I would fear that her Epoch could find any remaining stones and break her out, but her prison cell is enchanted against most magic. There's a light transport there as well, if you recall me telling you, but it's also outlawed, so we have to travel by ship now."

Liv sat next to Wes. "Why is the prison beyond the Harbor if it's so dangerous to pass through?"

Wes sighed. "Olan and Eljene's father started the build of the prison when they were children. Olan and my father finished it before the wars started thousands of years ago. It was the best place, because even if prisoners escaped, they would hardly stand a chance against the Harbor—nowhere to go, really. It's a single passage, many miles away from anything, without a ship it would be impossible to swim the distance. There's one island amidst all the dangers, closest to the prison, but the island is rumored to be pretty horrific as well. You'll see what I mean when we get to the prison. It's a horrible place guarded by terrible creatures."

Liv felt a knot in her stomach. "Sounds—fun." She said sarcastically. "Then, were the wars against other cities in Lysterium? Started by Umaro?"

Wes laughed. "No. The wars started long before Umaro fell to darkness. My grandfather, allied with another world called Darcerion, and started the wars. Darcerion is the only other planet in our solar system that can host life, but it's a desolate place, nothing like Lysterium. When he died Darcerion invaded for a second time." His countenance became somber as he looked down.

Liv sat up straighter and shifted her body more toward Wes. "So, there's *another* magical world! Wait, your grandfather was bad?"

"Yes, and yes. He ruled in the first and second age of Lysterium. He succumbed to the curse on our bloodline, turned dark and tried to enslave Lysterium, he even imprisoned the prophets. We lost a lot of good Lysterians. Unfortunately, Umaro followed the same path, but she *did* fight for good for many years."

Liv put her hand on his arm. "It sounds like a lot has happened to your family. A curse on your bloodline? Is it still there? Is that what Coralis was talking about when she said 'another'?"

Wes looked up. "The curse still plagues the bloodline but it's pretty specific, a lot to explain. It was a hard time for all of us. It's late, love. Who we lost is too long, and tragic of a story for tonight. It was a particularly difficult time for me, I don't really like talking about it."

She sighed. "Okay. What kind of people were you fighting?"

Wes scoffed. "People? Creatures. Imagine every horrible thing you can think of from a nightmare; that's what we fought against. Some of the creatures were captured by our side and turned by my family; they're the ones that guard the prison. Although they serve Lysterium, they're still extremely dangerous and not to be trusted. I really wish you didn't have to encounter them, but I'll keep you safe."

"It's scary to think of all the unknowns out there. I've only just discovered that Lysterium existed, and there's still so much to learn. Even just about my own husband! Let alone a second magical world I didn't know about."

Wes sighed wearily. "There are things here you'll wish you never had to meet or learn about." He rubbed his eyes.

Liv felt disquieted about having to cross paths with such beings. She scooted back on the bed, toward the pillow, and pulled the rich covers over her. Wes moved near her, resting his upper body against the headboard, she snuggled into his chest, and yawned as they sat in silence. He ran his fingers absently through her hair in deep thought until she fell asleep again.

C HAPTER 6
Pyxis

AFTER GETTING READY FOR THE new day, Liv met Wes in the great dining hall for breakfast. He was standing next to the largest table reading a book while taking a sip of coffee. She stopped to watch him for a moment; he was unaware she was there. He was dressed in a navy three-button vest with an untucked tan button-down shirt underneath, with the sleeves rolled up, and a pair of tailored brown herringbone pants. His glacial blue eyes and platinum hair caught beams of light coming through the window as he walked around the table, still reading, making him look positively delectable. She felt lucky that Wes loved her. It seemed they both felt better this morning.

Liv was feeling excited about finally seeing the long-awaited city of Pyxis. She felt as if bugs were swarming in her stomach with anticipation. Even more exciting, she would soon get to sail on a Lysterian ship. She had never been sailing. Thinking back, she realized it was most likely because the memories were too painful for her mother. "Good morning." She smiled and then looked around. "Where are Olan and Coralis?"

Wes looked up from his book. "Hi. You're up."

"Bright-eyed and bushy-tailed," she laughed.

His perfect teeth glistened as he smiled. He closed the book and set it on the table. "They had a city meeting. We'll see them a bit later. Are you hungry?"

Liv's stomach growled, and she realized she hadn't eaten since that bite of muffin the day before. "Starving!" She walked over and sat down at the table, which could have seated the entire royal family of Great Britain and then some. Before her was a glorious display of delicious food. "I've barely seen Icarus. Do you know where he is?"

"I'm sure he's out exploring. I wouldn't worry about him."

"I miss him," she said, reaching for a plate. She was delightfully overwhelmed by all the delectable choices. "Did you rest at all?"

Wes joined her, sipping from his mug. "Yes, I stayed with you all night, thinking, but I feel relaxed today. Did you sleep well, my love?"

She nodded as she took a bite of croissant and fig dipped in honey.

After breakfast, they found Icarus in the garden. He rolled in the grass and talked with Liv over by one of the tide pools while she drank her coffee. Wes was standing under a large willow tree and had a chat with Orelia. It was a lovely start to the day and just what they all needed: peace. They were set to meet Finn, the captain, in Pyxis soon. Wes flew them the back way so Liv could see the city from the dock entrance, which he said was the best way to see it for the first time.

As they approached the city, the worries Liv was harboring seemed to melt away for the moment. A cool breeze tousled her hair and chilled her ivory skin as they landed on the dock. The sky was clear that morning, dozens of ships were tied to the moorings, and water slapped and sloshed against them. Pyxis was the smallest city Liv had seen in Lysterium but it wasn't lacking in enchantment. It was one of the working regions, bustling with a heavy population of traders, captains, and merchants. The sounds of ships and voices resonated high into the atmosphere. The city was a peninsula, surrounded on three sides, by the glittering blue of the sea. The long dock stretched horizontally across the entrance to Pyxis. Men of all sorts were loading ships or rushing down the dock. Most of the women Liv could see were in the air. They all had glittering skin and small feathered wings on their ankles. As they flew past, their pastel-colored hair and unmatched beauty enthralled her.

Wes put his hand on her shoulder and pointed to one of the women. "They are the water nymphs."

Liv turned to look at him with gleaming eyes. Wes took her hand and started walking down the dock.

As if to herald their arrival, hundreds of massive sailboats were floating in midair, filling the sky. The waves of flourishing white sails danced like women's dresses in the wind. The men manning the ships appeared to have stepped right out of Valhalla. They wore decorated helmets with large silver wings, and their hefty chests were covered only by silver breastplates adorned with the same wings. More ships sailed on the water; some were entering the city, and others were leaving.

Liv whipped her head all around with wide eyes at every new view as they walked along the dock toward the entrance to the city. They saw a large black ship with white wings painted on the side, resting at the end of the dock, near the entrance. The fresh breeze rippled the massive sails, and leaning against a wooden post was a man. They walked toward him. He straightened as soon as he saw Liv and Wes approaching.

Wes gave a congenial head nod. "Good morning. I'm Wes, and this is Liv. Are you our captain through the Harbor?"

The man removed his brown newsboy hat and bowed slightly, causing his thick crop of sandy-blond hair to fall in a mess over his bright blue eyes, highlighting his crooked smile. He spoke fast with a heavy Irish accent "The name's Finnegan Riordan, at your service," he said, looking up with a cheerful grin. "Call me Finn." He winked. His attire suggested he was much older than he looked, and seemed a little worse for wear with his shabby, early nineteen-hundreds style. He pulled casually at the suspenders attached to the wide-legged trousers, in which his white T-shirt tucked, swaying slightly forward and backward in his work boots. He walked over to Liv and kissed her hand. "So I get ta' be sharin' me ship wi' such a pretty ting. We'll have some fun." He winked again, still holding her hand. Which caused Liv to blush.

Wes cleared his throat. "We're going to join you with gathering supplies, so Liv can see the city."

Finn straightened, replaced his hat, and nodded at Wes, but he was still looking at Liv with a hungry stare. "Oh, it's gonna be a good journey." He smiled, jumped onto his ship, and shouted from the deck, "Just grabbin' a few things, be right down."

Liv turned to Wes and laughed. "I see he's going to be trouble."

Wes eyed Finn. "Yes. You'll have to keep your defenses up; I have a feeling he is going to be quite persistent."

Finn returned to the dock momentarily with an empty burlap bag over his shoulder, and off they walked. At the end of the dock, they passed through enormous abalone gates, stepping onto a street made of crushed red coral that veered off in many directions. They took the main path, which led to a courtyard. There Liv could now see the towering golden women up close in all of their magnificence. Her mouth slightly open in awe at the level of detail. The fabric creased and folded as if it were moving, the skin on their bare feet was so lifelike Liv almost expected them to start walking. Even from the great height she noticed their waist length hair had every strand carved. She thought the sculptor must have been a magician or else there used to be giant women in Lysterium and they were preserved in liquid gold. Liv snickered to herself.

They walked through the courtyard, with Finn leading the way, and continued on the path, which was lined with large, draping willow trees that swayed romantically. There was always a constant breeze, being on the water, so willow flowers floated in the air all around like snow, filling the city, with golden feathers here and there floating among them. A faint scent of magnolia wafted in the air, but the smell of fish, and the salty sea were dense throughout the city.

Wes seemed to glow in the sunlight since his features were so fair. The breeze picked up the hem of Liv's pink-and-white patterned toile dress, and rippled it in all directions against her calves as she walked.

As they passed the row of willows, a market came into view. It was set up in a circle, split down the middle by the path, similar to a glorified fish market. Cobblestone sidewalks stemming from the main road led to the many shops lining each side of the circle. The shops were made of rustic knotted ash and beech wood, which showed the wear of time. It was busy; each shop was laden with products, and filled with customers.

Finn turned around. "We're headin' round the other side. I want the weapons shop."

The main path continued to the end of a cul-de-sac where the largest building in Pyxis resided; the meeting hall. This was the only building made of stone block, with large wooden double doors at the entrance. There were three windows on each side of the entrance, made of wavy green glass. The block had heavy moss in the seams, covering most of the building, due to the constant humidity of the sea. A golden bell hung on the outer wall, to the right of the entrance, with a canary carved on it and a small rope hanging from the bottom.

Directly to the left of the meeting hall was a great clock tower. The tower was ornate with bas relief carvings of winged women, ships, water, and filigree. The entire clock was outlined with a silver lace, and the face was twenty feet across, with intricate silver hands. Inside the right corner of the clock face, resided a smaller clock with only four symbols, one each in the twelve, three, six, and nine positions. Above the outside of the face, a series of metal birds in flight followed the curve of the clock. A small watchtower was settled above the clock, with a spiral staircase discreetly hidden to the side. The main clock, Liv noticed, was in minutes and hours, how Earth's time is displayed. This was the first-time Liv had seen a clock in a Lysterian city.

Liv was afraid to blink, for fear she might miss something. "Wes, what is that smaller clock, and why is the large one like Earth time?"

"Pyxis does a lot of trade with Earth. Although the human merchants don't know they are trading with goods from another world, many of the ships go back and forth daily. They have to keep to a schedule that is conducive with Earth. Most captains have a watch from Earth based on which time zone they deliver to. The main clock just helps remind the sailors of the vast time difference between us and Earth. The other clock is Lysterian time; it doesn't really measure by minutes or hours, since our days are much longer. Rather, it measures the shifts of a day: morning, afternoon, evening, and overnight."

"Hmm." Liv processed the information.

Finn was far ahead of them. "Keep up, will ya?"

To the left of the clock tower was a smaller path, more discreet. Finn took it, and soon they were coming to a pier that led to the open sea again. The pier, only fifty feet long, was built high into the air. The sea far below was washing over the white sand. Near the end were two small shops nestled across from each other. Wes mentioned they were the first shops built in Pyxis; one was an apothecary, and the other a weapon shop. They planned to go to both.

The apothecary shop was packed with glass vials of all shapes and sizes filled with medicines, potions, and remedies. Many rows of books, herbs, scales, and devices Liv didn't recognize filled the remainder of the shop. Finn had ordered several different items, and as he was talking to the owner, Liv had an idea.

She came to a small section containing empty vials and picked up three of them. Then a thought occurred to her. She walked over to Wes. "What's the currency in Lysterium?"

"There is no currency. In Lysterium, there isn't a need for it. Each ruler takes care of his or her people. Everyone is provided for; most shops trade for what they need or want."

Liv was baffled. "Trade? How does that work? What about living expenses and such?"

Wes laughed. "Darling, this isn't Earth. Currency isn't necessary."

She held up the vials. "Well, then how do I get these?"

"Just tell the shopkeeper what you want. I'm a royal, so it's not a problem."

Liv frowned at playing the royal card. "I'd like to pay for them."

Unfortunately, she was met with disappointment when the shopkeeper wouldn't let her give him anything for the vials.

When they left the apothecary, they headed for the weapons shop, which was lined wall to wall with all sorts of weapons and gadgets. She walked around, amazed at all the strange things in the shop. It was like a general store, but the merchandise was deadly: strange swords, what Liv could only assume were bow-and-arrow contraptions, metal nets, and devices that made temporary wings, which Liv had experienced in Umaro's dungeon. She walked over to a section that had hundreds of compasses, all of them serving different functions aside from just direction. In the back of the shop was a small section of potions different from the apothecary's. These potions provided temporary strengths and powers. Liv picked some of them up to read the contents: "Extra limbs. Laceration powder. Decapitation elixir." Liv put her hand on her throat and swallowed. Then she came across one that intrigued her: "Siren's song." She looked at it with curious eyes.

She walked over to the shopkeeper. "Excuse me, sir. What does this do?" She held the vial up.

As the shopkeeper turned to face her, she saw he was far from human. Liv felt his appearance was frightful. His red eyes glinted in the sun's reflection, and his long, thin dark grayish face, with a white handlebar mustache and goatee, curled into a welcoming grin of sharp teeth. He was gaunt and worn looking, almost skeletal.

His sandpaper voice was raspy. "Not often I get a pretty human in my shop," he said politely. His speech sounded similar to a pirate's. He pointed to the vial Liv was holding up. "That there is a must-have on the open sea."

She was relieved he was kind. "What does it do exactly?"

"Well, you see, miss, there ain't no potion in the worlds that can fight off Sirens; they're too strong and cunning. So, I created this one to help win favor with 'em. It only works for a short while, but if ye get captured, it will stall the killin'. I've had a few sailors come back sayin' they were captured and made it out alive only because of this here potion." He beamed at Liv with a clear confidence that he had created something amazing.

"Oh! What can I trade for it?" Liv asked, hoping this time she could give the shopkeeper something.

His smile shifted to nervous and he stalled, then shyly spoke this time. "I would ask for one thing, if it ain't too much trouble."

Liv straightened and widened her eyes. "What is it?" she said upbeat, happy she could trade.

He looked down and fumbled with his hands. "I would like—a kiss."

Liv's smile faded, and her heart sank. The shopkeeper put his hands up, his gray skin turning red. "Not on the lips or nothin', just on the cheek. I rarely ever see humans, and the ones I do see ain't half as pretty as you. It would brighten me day to know I had a kiss from ye." He didn't look scary at all anymore; instead, he looked like a hopeful child.

Liv shrugged. "Well, since you put it so flatteringly."

She leaned over the counter, which made the old shopkeeper flinch, and kissed his cheek. His eyes turned a brighter red, and his skin seemed to glow.

He closed his eyes. "Thank you, miss. I haven't been touched in years." He put his hand on the spot she had kissed. Liv suddenly felt incredibly sad. Everyone needed to be touched and loved. *How awful*, she thought, *that no one has shown him affection.*

She walked around the counter and opened her arms. The shopkeeper looked at her with confusion. Liv rolled her hands toward her with her arms still open. "Free hug," she said, smiling.

Liv noticed he had a bad limp as he slowly walked over and sank into the hug. Liv, on her tip toes to reach, held on to him, speaking softly in his ear. "Everyone needs affection from time to time."

The sweet moment lingered, and Liv felt warm and glad she had something to give to this creature. When they finally let go, Liv saw that the shopkeeper had a tear falling down his cheek.

He turned away from Liv and started cleaning some compasses. "Thank you," he whispered, not looking at her.

She put her hand on his shoulder for a second and then walked out of the shop with her potion. She stared out at the sea, leaning against the dock, thinking about the poor shopkeeper. Finn and Wes walked out a few minutes later, their arms full of supplies and Finn's sack bursting.

Wes walked over to Liv. "What was that about?"

"What?"

"You know, the hug. Was he all right? I know I lived on Earth for many years, but human behavior still baffles me sometimes. It's enjoyable to witness these strange customs."

Liv loved how accepting Wes was. "It makes me so sad. He said that no one had touched him in years. Isn't that awful? To not be shown any kind of affection—in years! I couldn't bear it."

Wes slid his free arm around her shoulders and squeezed. "I love you." He smiled. "You've always had a good heart."

When they arrived back at the ship, they put away the supplies, then Liv and Wes said good-bye to Finn, as they headed back to Harp Isle.

"See ya!" Finn called, waving his hat in the air as they flew off.

Liv was in a dreamlike state from all the beauty of Pyxis. "I've decided this is where we need to live."

Wes gave her a scolding look. "Hey, I'm the ruler of Elderwood. Don't make that decision until you've at least *seen* my region!" He pretended to be offended, and then snickered.

"Okay, okay, good point. But still, I love it here."

"I think you'll love Elderwood. It's very different. I'm admittedly partial, but it's my favorite region."

The corners of Liv's eyes creased with joy. "I'm sure it's incredible if you rule it. I hope I get to see it soon."

Wes lowered them to the front door, by the time they arrived at Harp Isle, the sun was high in the sky. Since the days were much longer, it only appeared to be midday; however, they had been out for hours, viewing the city and stocking the ship. To their surprise, Eljene, Amara, and Chauncy, Wes's father, were gathered with Olan and Coralis in the dining hall.

Olan looked up, noticing them. "Oh, good, you're back. I've assembled a meeting; I think it will be safer to have all of us together. Westy, come in here. We're making plans for when we arrive at the prison."

Liv looked up at Wes. "I don't think I need to sit in on this one. I'm just going to be a passenger on the journey. I think I'll go in the great room and relax for a little while, if that's okay?"

"Of course, I shouldn't be too long." Since Wes towered over Liv, he kissed the crown of her head, and then he walked toward the others as she left the room.

She was relieved to get out of that conversation; she knew that most of their meeting was going to be a lecture on safety. Then the topic of her not going would come up, yet again. She wasn't up for arguing. She had enjoyed a lovely day seeing Pyxis and wanted to relax. She went upstairs and changed out of her dress. She figured they would all have dinner together, so she threw on some jeans and a cotton tank top. To have a hint of formality, she added a fitted vertical-striped jacket, which she left open, and black calf-length wool boots.

She made her way back down to the great room. She flipped through some books on the shelves until she came across one that piqued her interest. It was titled *The Wars' History: Volume 1.* She tucked it under her arm and walked toward the dining hall. She could hear raised voices at the meeting—mostly Olan and Eljene, because they were naturally loud. She peeked her head around the corner to make sure the discussion wasn't getting too heated. The meeting centered on safety strategies and carefully planned routes, as she'd thought it would. Recalling Wes's description of the creatures guarding the prison, she felt a twinge of nerves. And if the guards were that scary, then what were the prisoners like? She sighed.

Liv hadn't yet seen the kitchen, and when she rounded the corner from the dining room, she stood in awe at how large and well stocked it was. Huge, knotty wooden cabinets lined all the walls, and two enormous ovens were covered with pots and pans simmering and roasting away. There were big sacks of grains and vegetables in one corner, and barrels of fruit and hanging meats filled the opposite corner. In the center, bustling around, was a chef wearing an apron bearing the signature wings of Pyxis.

"Pardon me, sir," she said quietly.

The chef, who was humming to himself, turned casually. "Oh yes, hello, madam. How can I help you?" He had a handlebar mustache and blond hair peeking out of his hat.

"I was just wondering if I could maybe get a snack."

Liv knew that Lysterian's were generous, but she hadn't expected to leave the kitchen with a basket full of breads, jams, fruit, chocolate, and nuts. She was nonetheless delighted, because her trip to the city had worked up an appetite, and she didn't know how long the others would be in the meeting. She retreated to the great room with the book still under her arm and the basket in her other hand.

She sat down in a high-backed chair near the fire, picked some of the delicious food out of the basket, and began to eat. When she was done, she set the basket on a side table and flipped through the book, excited to learn some of the history that yet eluded her. She tucked her legs up on the chair and let her body loosen. Within a few minutes, the book slid out of her hand as she fell asleep, full, warm, and weary from the day.

CHAPTER 7
A Garish Nightmare

LIV WOKE WITH A VIOLENT jerk. She didn't know how long she had been asleep, and lately, she'd had nothing but nightmares. She wiped under her eyes for makeup residue, picked up the book that had fallen out of her lap and placed it on the side table. The basket of food was still there, so she plucked some grapes from it. As she ate the crisp, sweet grapes she stared blankly at the fire, letting it lull her back into a relaxed state. As she watched, the fire seemed to grow taller and more ferocious. Liv dropped her legs down from the chair and leaned closer. Red smoke was forming a sphere in the height of the flames. She blinked slowly and looked again; an envelope materialized in the fire. She drew back, frightened at first, but then curious. The envelope hovered for a moment in the flames and then quickly shot out, landing at her feet.

She jumped back, dropping the few grapes she had left, and then noticed that the letter had her name on it. She stared at it, remembering the last time an envelope had appeared this way. She reached down, flipped it over, and saw Umaro's red seal. She broke the seal with trepidation and removed the parchment; her hands shook slightly as she unfolded the letter and saw the familiar handwriting, slanted and elegant, in black ink.

I have decided to hasten your arrival to my squalid prison. You will come to me alone; I will know if any of my family is with you. I suggest you not test me in this. Enclosed is a modified vanishing stone that will take you directly to the outskirts of the prison. When you are ready to travel, throw it hard at the ground. If you do not come, or if you bring anyone with you, I will kill your father.

U.

Liv studied the letter with the same shock she'd felt upon reading Umaro's first letter. She read it several times. She started to breathe heavily, so much so, that she felt light-headed. As she folded the letter and went to put it back, a golf-ball-sized red jewel appeared inside the envelope. It looked like a large garnet, deep in color, glittering and beautiful. Liv turned the vanishing stone over in her hand and despondently considered what she ought to do. She knew with certainty that everyone would oppose her going, but she couldn't let Umaro murder her father. Liv knew that Umaro was perfectly capable of sending an Epoch or something worse to kill Lucian; it seemed Umaro was the only one who knew his location.

Liv's heart pounded. She checked that her watch was safely tucked inside her shirt. She buttoned her jacket and looked around the room until she saw what she was after.

The first time Liv had entered the great room, she had noticed a sheath of daggers nestled on a shelf full of compasses and maps. She checked the door. Seeing that the hall was empty, she walked over to the bookcase and picked up the sheath that held four ornate, sharp daggers tucked neatly into individual slots. She stowed it inside her right boot, and put one of the compasses in her jacket pocket. She looked around for anything else that might be useful. She found a map of the Harbor, with details of the prison, and tucked that in her other boot. She walked back over to the chair she had been sitting in and picked up the letter, unfolding it. She placed it face up on the chair so that Wes would see it. She took a pen off of the desk and wrote on the bottom of the letter; the difference in their writing contrasted on the page.

I'm so sorry, but I can't let anyone else die for me. I had to go. It's better this way.

I love you.

Her shaking hands gripped the vanishing stone as she took a deep breath. Her heart pounded ferociously and almost visibly against her shirt. Her stomach lurched as she threw the stone hard at the ground near her feet. Bright light and thick red mist surrounded her as a ghostly, seemingly distant scream, rose up and out. She felt a sensation of pulling, as if her body were being split into a thousand pieces. She gritted her teeth and held her breath. A second later, something sharp was digging into her leg.

Don't scream. They'll hear, she told herself, clenching her jaw. It was a horrible feeling. Just when she thought she couldn't take it any longer, her feet were on land.

Liv swayed forward with the impact of the landing, feeling queasy and trying to steady herself. She was standing on a long stretch of wet, dark greenish-black cobblestone covered in moss and grime. Then she saw him: Icarus was shaking his head and trying to gain balance.

She cried out, "Icarus! What are you doing here?" She squatted down and stared with equal feelings of worry and relief that she wasn't alone.

"I saw the letter shoot out from the fireplace. When you threw the vanishing stone, I knew I had to follow you. Mother what are you doing? This is dangerous." He looked around and shuddered. "The prison? Alone?"

"Listen, I had to go. She was threatening to kill Lucian. I didn't have a choice." She picked him up as she stood. "I'm glad you're here with me, but you have to—"

Her voice was stayed as she lifted her eyes from the ground.

She stared out at the sea. It wasn't like the glittering beauty she had seen earlier in the city; this was menacing and frightful. The Harbor had an eerie green veil of haze and stretched as far as Liv could see. Immeasurable precipitous, jagged cliffs walled the water into a charade of a harbor. Pieces of skeletal ships floated aimlessly in the brackish water, moving with the waves. She felt fear's icy grip come over her, and too late, she wondered how she was going leave this place, having already used the only vanishing stone.

Gripping Icarus tighter, she turned around. A few yards up, the cobblestone path continued onto a massive bridge, also made of stone. The canyon, Liv could see to either side of the bridge, was nothing but dark emptiness thousands of feet deep, and somewhere beyond the long-stretching bridge lay the prison.

"All right, this is the scariest place I've ever been to." She tried to laugh. "Icarus, you have to stay here. God knows what's up there! I can't lose you. I just can't. I'll see Umaro and then come get you, and we'll find a way to get out of here, okay?"

Icarus looked upset. Liv knew he would want to make sure she was safe, but the terrified look in her eyes seemed to convince the cat to agree to remain behind. "Be smart, don't let her trick you. And stay safe!"

"I will. Don't go near the water, and stay hidden," Liv whispered as she gave Icarus another hug before setting him down. She looked behind her one last time, giving him a meek wave, and then she made her approach toward the prison.

The air was dense and humid, with an odor of decay lingering. Everything was wet from the sea air and constant storms. Liv was terrified, but there was no turning back; she had to go in and face whatever Umaro had planned. She walked toward the bridge. She was not a fan of heights; the never-ending appearance of the vastness under the bridge kept her tense. She walked directly in the middle, so as not to see the edge, and moved as fast as she could without stumbling over the uneven stone. The bridge seemed to go on forever. She held her arms tightly around herself to stave off the violent trembling.

Her mouth gaped as she reached the end of the bridge and saw the prison masquerading as a great castle. Charred stone made up the walls, and the building was so tall that Liv could not see the top, because it was enveloped by dark clouds. Creeping thorny vines covered the walls of the dungeon, and large blackbirds circled constantly around the structure. The prison, it seemed, had been carved right out of a mountain, with nothing but cliffs of razor-sharp rock surrounding it. She slapped her hand over her gaping mouth in horror. Near the entrance were large spears sticking out of the ground with impaled decaying bodies. Large cages hung over the cliffs, suspended by rusted chains. The bodies, and distorted faces hanging out of them, were in various stages of decomposition. Birds picked at the bones of the dead. Liv couldn't imagine there being a place like this in Lysterium. Even some of the more frightening places, such as Torr, still held intense beauty. This was nothing like that; it was truly horrifying, as if she had entered the land of the dead—and she didn't have a way out.

The entrance to the prison was a series of protected gates. The first was a daunting drawbridge made of iron, in the down position. As Liv stepped onto the iron, the air became colder. She pulled at her jacket as she continued the long walk forward. The wind picked up as she made her way to the second gate, wafting up a salty mildew with undertones of rot. Her boots dropped down as she left the iron and made contact with the cobblestone path again. The second gate was open as well. It was a grid of small hollow iron squares with large spikes sticking out, and it had an enormous keyhole that was rusted and simple. Finally, after a long walk, Liv approached the main doors, which were solid black iron and stood a menacing three stories high.

Two terrifying creatures flanked the enormous doors. Liv gripped her stomach as she fought to keep from vomiting, acid from the grapes crept up her throat. It felt like a nightmare—the atmosphere, the tortured corpses, and now true monsters.

They stood as tall as three men standing on each other's shoulders and had faces that looked like mutated boars, with hollow white eyes, and large tusks curving upward out of their bottom lips. Their grotesquely fat bodies were motionless, but their skin looked like melted wax dripping, which made them almost ripple. They had giant bloody blades in place of forearms; the melted skin oozed over the blades where they began at the elbow. They were shirtless, their upper arms cuffed in iron that dug into their skin, and large iron belts decorated with real human skulls held up their tattered pants.

Liv's entire body trembled as she approached the creatures. When they saw her, they made a terrible mechanical-sounding noise and deeply inhaled to catch her scent. They came toward her in a hostile manner, drawing up their bladed arms, and glowering at her. Liv stopped and slowly started stepping backward.

One of the creatures spoke in a booming, yet piggish squeal. "What is your purpose, human?"

Liv webbed her fingers together in an attempt to stop the shaking. She looked up with huge eyes. "I—" She swallowed hard and blinked, squeezing her eyes shut momentarily. "I'm here to question a prisoner," she said with an uncontrollably shaking voice.

The creature that had not spoken, leaned over and sniffed Liv with a rasping growl. It looked up at the other and then said, "The human is clear of magic. Enter."

Liv looked up. "Th-th-thank you." She walked past them with an even pace, telling herself every moment not to run. To her relief, the doors started to open, and she stepped inside. The moment she entered, the doors started to close slowly, shutting out the terrible creatures that lay on the other side. She leaned over and dry heaved, holding her stomach. She had never felt so scared in her life, not even when she was captured by the Epoch. Wes had been right; there were things she wished she hadn't encountered.

The air inside the dungeon was foul and stale. The sounds of dripping water, and wailing in the distance, echoed hauntingly throughout the prison, unsettling her nerves. The dungeon had flights and flights of stairs that spiraled up to different levels with cells on both sides. Everything was made of stone and iron, except for one humble door, made of wood to the right of the entrance. There was a small sign on the door that said simply, Watcher. Liv walked over to the door and knocked once meekly. She saw the doorknob turning, a beautiful woman with glimmering ebony skin answered. Liv's body relaxed. The woman's winged feet and lavender hair revealed that she was from Pyxis. Her face was kind but looked worn and tired from years at a hard post.

When she saw Liv, she seemed surprised. "I am the watcher of this prison. What is your business?" she said politely, but with authority.

Liv was under the impression this woman was intimidating when she needed to be, and she appreciated her kindness in this instance. "My name is Liv. My husband is Weston from Elderwood. I'm here to question Umaro."

The watcher moved toward Liv, resting her hand on the door frame, as if to block it. "Umaro is a high-security prisoner. I cannot allow visitors." She was still kind, but sterner now that she knew Liv's intentions.

Liv's face fell into pleading. "Please. She has information on a victim. It's a matter of life and death. I *have* to talk to her."

"What victim would this be?"

Liv debated whether or not to tell her the truth, and decided the truth was always better. "My father," she said plainly.

The watcher dropped her hand from the door, and her body relaxed slightly at Liv's candor. Liv saw her face soften and continued, "I received a letter from Umaro. She has my father, and she said that if I didn't come to her, she would kill him. So, you understand why I must see her."

"This is high security; I would need to speak with Olan before allowing it."

Liv turned pale. She pleaded again, "Please. I was with Olan. My husband and I were planning a journey here to see the prisoner under Olan's orders."

The watcher looked intently at her. "Then where is the rest of your company?"

Liv swallowed. "Plans changed, and I needed to come alone—please."

The watcher paused for what seemed a long time, and then walked back into her office and taking something out of a drawer. "I can only give you a few moments with her," she said, sounding doubtful.

Liv's face lit up. "Oh, thank you! That should suffice."

The watcher nodded at Liv. "Follow me. This prison is for the truly evil and deranged, so there are some rules we need to cover." She spoke in a monotone voice, as if she had recited these words thousands of times. "Don't make eye contact with any prisoner. Don't get close to any prisoner. You must stand at least four feet from the bars at all times, and absolutely do not approach the guards."

Liv nodded. "Yes, ma'am. Um—are the guards the same as those scary things outside?"

The watcher smiled. "No, they only guard the outer gates."

Liv's shoulders dropped dramatically as she felt relief wash over her. "Thank God. Those are the scariest things I've ever seen! What are they?"

"They are the Mutilatus. They were created by the Darcerion during the great wars. They were cursed, tortured, and disfigured into the creatures that you see. Only a few are left in Lysterium. We were able to persuade those few to pledge loyalty to us after the wars. I wouldn't linger near them. They are ruthless and wouldn't think twice about savagely tearing anyone to pieces. Most unpleasant, but they do their job well here" She shrugged.

Liv swallowed hard and wrapped her arms around her ribs. "Well, I'm going to have nightmares for the rest of my life, I think." She let out a little nervous laugh.

As they walked up the outstretched maze of stairs, Liv could see hundreds of prison cells. Some of the prisoners were hostile, and lashed out through the bars, in an attempt to grab Liv. Others screamed or made disturbing comments, and some tried to bribe Liv as she passed. She was walking so close to the watcher, to keep safe, that she was practically stepping on her. None of this seemed to faze the watcher; she was likely used to this place and behaviors.

After about seventeen flights of stairs, Liv paused, panting heavily, and bent over, clutching her ribs. Although she was thin, and taut, she was not an exerciser. "I need a break. Don't you have an elevator?" She gasped for air.

The watcher, unaffected by the hike, stared at Liv with an expression of amusement. "Humans." She rolled her eyes.

Liv felt disgruntled. "It's a lot of stairs! Give me a break, would you? How many more flights do we have to go?" She prayed for only a few.

The watcher was casual. "Twenty-five."

Liv grimaced, letting out a frustrated shriek. "Aw!" she whined, still gripping the stitch in her side.

"You asked to see the prisoner with the highest security; she is held in the top cell."

Liv looked up, still panting. "I didn't know what I was getting myself into. If I had, I would have tried to snag one of those armband wing thingies."

The watcher looked at Liv with a bewildered face, it appeared she wasn't accustomed to humans, then she put her arm around Liv's waist. "You'd better hold on." She lifted Liv off the ground. She was so fast in flight that Liv jerked back at the acceleration, which caused her to make a strange gurgling sound, as she was unable to find her breath.

In a matter of seconds, they were at the top tower. The watcher spoke as she set Liv down. "I'm afraid you will have to walk the last flight; her guards take over from here."

Liv started patting down her wild curls. "Thank you so much. I think you just saved my life!"

The watcher smiled and shrugged. "I will be waiting here for you. Remember, do not approach the guards. When you are finished, just walk down the steps to this point. And keep your distance from the bars—at least four feet. I assume you have a watch?"

Liv patted her chest and nodded.

"Good. You have ten minutes from the time you reach the cell. Good luck."

"Thank you." Liv smiled and ascended the stairs. The narrow curve of the stairs was so tight that Liv couldn't see what was coming next until she was already turning.

When she reached the top, her stomach dropped as she saw the guards. They were not as bad as the Mutilatus, but were still dreadful. Two of them stood at the mouth of the stairs, about fifteen feet from the cell. Each had the body of a man but what appeared to be the head of a raven. Long, sharp beaks protruded far out of slotted, tight-fitting black helmets with large black feathers sticking out of the top. Bits of bone were tied around the feathers, and their eyes were covered. They wore black Victorian pants and shiny chainmail shirts that looked like scales. Their sharp, unnaturally long, pointed claws were covered by heavy gloves made of the same scaly metal. Liv could hear their rattled breathing as she passed by. Their heads followed her. She made certain not to look at them.

In all her years, Liv had never seen creatures as terrible as some of the ones she had encountered in Lysterium, first in Torr and now here. She felt disquieted that she had come across such a gruesome part of this world. For all of its beauty, Lysterium held secret terrors that lurked in the various regions, waiting to consume victims. There was still much that Liv didn't know about Lysterium, which made her feel small and vulnerable. She was married to a royal, yet she knew nothing about the wars or the secrets they seemed to have hidden in every corner. Lysterium was still a mystery, as was her own past, which she couldn't quite reach. Perhaps Umaro, even if she had some machination, would tell Liv something about her father, and could give her some answers.

CHAPTER 8
Umaro's Plot

LIV CLEARED HER MIND, AND tried to focus on what she needed to get out of Umaro. She couldn't afford to let her emotions take over. Umaro would expect that of her after last time, and use it to her advantage. She slowly stepped toward the cell; it was dark, cold, and quiet. She couldn't see where Umaro was positioned.

Out of the depths of the cell came Umaro's threatening voice. "You see, a little persuasion goes a long way."

Liv stopped walking and let her eyes focus on the darkness of the cell. The faint light from the tiny window in the cell revealed Umaro's position: her shadowed outline was perched in the corner, illuminated only by her glowing burgundy eyes.

"Where's my father?" Liv demanded, willing herself to keep her voice steady and strong.

Umaro stood slowly. Just as her hourglass silhouette appeared in the dim cell, Liv saw Umaro moving closer. She slid her hands seductively around the bars, her elbows bent. Her long fingers tapped against the iron over and over, as if she were bored. Suddenly, Umaro's head appeared in the light as she pressed herself forward against the bars. Liv flinched.

Umaro was as beautiful as ever, but she looked run down. Her thick scarlet hair was pulled back in a loose braid with frizzy pieces of hair falling down the sides of her face and back. Dark circles showed through her fading makeup, but her burgundy eyes still glistened with bright beauty. Liv noticed that Umaro was thinner; her cheekbones were more prominent than the last time she had seen her.

A wide, frightful smile crept over Umaro's red lips as she took in the sight of Liv. "I can see you shaking."

Liv did not falter. "Where is he, Umaro?"

"Aw, she doesn't want to play. Patience, little Liv," with a cruel edge she teased.

Liv's face was getting hot. She didn't want to lose control, but Umaro was quickly consuming her imperturbability.

Umaro spoke in a falsely sweet voice. "Come closer, and I will tell you."

Liv took one step closer; she was about three feet from the bars.

"Closer. I want to see your pretty face when I'm speaking to you."

She knew Umaro wouldn't tell her anything unless she complied. She also knew Umaro had a trick up her sleeve, and Liv didn't want to fall into her trap. She moved another step closer. "This is the closest I'll come, until you give me some information—unless you don't really have any at all," she added snidely.

Umaro smiled again. "So, kitty does know how to play. Very well." She pulled a coin from her pocket and flicked it at Liv.

Liv caught it, to her relief. She looked it over, turning it to see both sides. It was the size of a silver dollar. A Lysterian language Liv couldn't read was carved all around the outer edges of both sides. In the center of one side of the coin was a tree, and on the other was a lion's head.

Liv was annoyed. "Is this supposed to mean something to me?"

Umaro's smile widened. "It's an exchange. That coin is a map to where your father is. To activate the map, you have to speak the words around the coin. You give me something, and I'll give you the inscription."

Liv stared at the coin and then back at Umaro. "I haven't seen a map like this in Lysterium. How do I know I can trust you?"

"The things you don't know could fill a library, you useless human!" Umaro's voice was angry for a moment, and then her smile came creeping back. "Or I suppose I should call you a half-breed."

Liv's eyes flickered. "What?"

Umaro laughed. "Oh, this is delicious! You don't know anything, do you?"

"If mocking me with meaningless garbage is all you have to say, then I'm leaving."

Umaro rolled her eyes. "It's a map that you can make yourself. The coin is enchanted. It's easier than carrying a large map and is easily hidden if necessary. The method was created during the wars by my cousin and I, to throw off the enemy. I have created this map with detailed instructions on how to find your father. Once the words are spoken, it'll show you and tell you what you need to do. I promise."

Liv sneered, "I can just ask Wes to read it for me."

Umaro cackled and shook her head mockingly.

Liv's cheeks were turning red. "What's that supposed to mean?"

"That's not how coin maps work. Eljene is a genius—do you really think she would invent something for use in a war, that anyone could decode? Only the maker can give the cypher to others, and then it can be read." Umaro's face was cunning.

"I can't trust you. You'll have to show me proof before I consent to anything. And speaking of, what do you want in return?"

Umaro stepped away from the light, folding her hands together and pacing near the bars. "Oh, just a small token, really. Nothing you'll miss."

Umaro's tone was unnerving, and Liv's heart jumped.

"I want, in exchange for your last family member's life and rescue"—she paused, letting it torment Liv. "—a vial of your blood."

Liv gave Umaro a horrified look. "So you can use the blood-oath vial against me? I don't think so!"

Umaro let out a shrill laugh that chilled Liv's blood. "I destroyed the blood-oath vial, or had you not figured that out yet?"

"I knew, but who knows what you did with it?" Liv retorted.

Umaro held her arm up with the palm facing Liv. There was an angry bloody burn in the center of her palm, blistering down her forearm. Her eyes glinted with rage. "My nephew used old magic to make that oath; it was more difficult to break than I had anticipated." Umaro regained composure and folded her hands together again. "Now, do we have a deal?" she said hungrily.

Liv felt acidic vomit creeping into her throat again. She could only imagine what Umaro wanted to do with her blood. On the other hand, could she let her father die because she valued her own life more? She was torn and anxious. "What are you going to do with my blood?" Liv demanded.

Umaro's voice was sickeningly sugary. "Ah, that wasn't part of the deal."

Liv felt cornered. "I can't just give you my blood and have you use some dark spell or something to kill me. How would that benefit me or my father? You evil—"

Umaro cut her off. "Now, now, play nice." She laughed. Liv grunted, and Umaro continued. "Look, I will give you the paper with the words to open the map. Finding your daddy is only a few steps away." She held up a small piece of parchment and waved it in the air.

Tears prickled in Liv's eyes. "I'm sorry. I can't endanger everyone around me; it would be selfish. I want to find my father but not at the cost of Lysterium." Liv slid the coin in her jacket pocket and turned to walk away.

Umaro gave her a steely look. "You should have taken the easy way," she said maliciously. "Do you really think I would let you just walk away after all my efforts to get you here? I will get what I want from you! I tried to be civil."

Without warning, Umaro force-pushed Liv into one of the guards. Liv crashed into him hard, knocking them both over. Liv looked up in terror. The watcher's warning repeated in her head: *Do not approach the guards.* A deep, predatory growl came from the raven-like creature. Liv's mouth dropped open as she stared at the giant claw rising in the air. The other guard had blocked the stairs, so she had nowhere to run. The hand came down with ferocity, knocking Liv into the bars of the cell. She was on the ground, leaning against them, stunned from the blow. Four deep gashes streaked her face where the claw had made contact. Warm sticky liquid dripping down her neck told Liv that her head was bleeding severely. Her face throbbed. She was dizzy and scrambling to stand, but couldn't get her footing.

The guard walked toward her, "That's enough of you." Umaro said coolly, flicking her wrist. He was suddenly thrown into the other guard, and both of them went tumbling down the stairs. Before Liv could comprehend what had happened, a bony hand reached around, gripped her jaw, and another hand pressed something sharp against her neck. Umaro pulled Liv's head against the bars with great force. Liv's legs flailed violently as she fought to get away, but Umaro was too strong. Liv tried to reach for the daggers in her boot, but with her head held captive, she couldn't manage. Weakened by the guard, she did the only thing she could think of: she started screaming for the watcher.

Umaro slammed Liv's head against the bars. "Shut your mouth!"

Liv's head pounded from the multitude of traumas, and her vision was blurring. Umaro turned Liv's face to the side, pushing her cheek into the bars, and whispered in her ear, "You should have known I would get what I wanted. This could have been much easier for you if you had just cooperated." Umaro slid the piece of parchment down Liv's shirt. Liv convulsed at the sensation of the bony fingers sliding down her flesh. "A deal's a deal," Umaro said. She callously wiped the blood from Liv's head with her hand. "Pity. I need an artery." Her steely eyes glowed red with excitement as she plunged a large needle resembling an embalming apparatus deep into Liv's neck and drew out the dark arterial blood.

Liv screamed. The needle remained deeply embedded. Umaro drenched her hands in the flowing blood and then kicked Liv down away from the bars. Liv gripped the needle, jerked it out of her neck, and applied pressure to stop the bleeding. Just then, the watcher came barreling up the stairs, followed by the guards. She saw Liv on the ground bleeding and then looked over at Umaro. A swirling black circle of smoke was forming in the cell, and a great book appeared in Umaro's hand. Liv, still gripping her neck, crawled farther away from the bars.

The watcher fumbled for keys. "Stop!"

Liv turned to face Umaro and gasped as she saw the book take form. "No! She has the Book of Prophecy!" Liv screamed at the watcher while reaching for the bars. Umaro gave Liv a malevolent smile, winked, and smeared the blood in the open pages.

A vast blackbird made of smoke rose out of the book. Umaro raised the open book over her head as the bird let out a deafening raucous screech so loud it was blinding.

Umaro laughed. "Couldn't have done it without you. See you soon."

Liv's eyes grew huge. "No!"

Umaro slammed the book closed, and the cell exploded into rubble. Liv raised her arms over her face as the shock waves of the blast hit her, and fire erupted like a cloud throughout the cell. Liv looked at the watcher as the blast blew her into the stone wall of the tower. Flames, debris, and rubble rained down on her. Her screams were muffled as she was engulfed.

The explosion was catastrophic, obliterating the tower. Liv was buried under a mountain of broken stone. In the explosion, a boulder had landed on top of her calves pinning her face down on her stomach where she fell. She tried to bury her face as the fire spread. She clawed at the ground in an attempt to free herself from the debris. As the fire died out, the dust and smoke was suffocating, rising into the dark sky. The stairwell was jammed with large pieces of stone and metal, so the only way out was up, but that wasn't an option. Liv's body was broken, trapped. Struggling to free herself, choking on smoke and dizzy with blood loss, she fell unconscious. Umaro was gone.

CHAPTER 9
Consequences

LIV SLOWLY OPENED HER EYES. They burned, and everything was blurry. Most of the smoke had cleared through the gaping opening in the roof. As she lifted her head, her hair was heavy, matted with blood and dirt. She could barely feel her legs. She coughed painfully. "Watcher?"

Shaking her head, Liv moved the pieces of debris within her reach and searched what she could see of the wreckage for the watcher. The watcher's boots were sticking out from under a large chunk of the mangled cell door. She shouted, "Oh God! Are you okay?"

Liv pulled herself up onto her elbow and strained to move the piece of door. When she had finally cleared the door away, her face was expressionless with shock. The watcher had been impaled by a piece of the cell bars. Her arms were spread out, and her eyes were wide and empty. Liv's heart broke. "I'm so sorry," she cried.

The weight of the stone crushing her legs was too heavy and wouldn't budge. She thought if she could get one leg free, she could use it to free the other one. In her attempts, she let out screams of agony, but she did not prevail in freeing herself. She laid her head on the ground and closed her eyes, fearing this would be her end. The night sky was black, and thick gray clouds loomed overhead. The air was growing cold and damp, and small fires still burned in the area where the cell had been. Her face was taut with swelling and pulsed with her heartbeats; her head throbbed, and she tasted copper and dirt.

It seemed as if hours had passed. She was alone, cold, and left with the agony of her terrible decision to come to the prison, which had inevitably aided Umaro in her escape. This had been Umaro's plan, but had she intended for Liv to die in the blast as well? *Two birds*, Liv thought. She hoped for death to arrive and put her out of her misery; the physical pain was extreme and ongoing, yet her shame hurt worse. Liv closed her eyes as the mildew and dust filled her senses. She laid her cheek on the ground and gave up. She lay for a long time in silence, when she heard a noise coming from the stairwell. She could hear bits of rubble being cleared away.

Then a voice shouted, "Is anyone alive?"

Liv raised her head. She could barely see through the dirt, blood, and dizziness of her trauma. Slowly, she propped herself up on her elbows and shouted as loudly as she could, which, in her state, was barely above a whisper, "Hello? Can you hear me? Please, I need help." Liv could hear the moving of debris become quicker and more frantic.

"Almost through. Just hold on."

The voice was male. Something seemed familiar about it. A large piece of the cell door had obstructed the hall. Liv saw it fly across the open room and land where the cell had once been. She heard footsteps, and then the man appeared in the entryway of the stairs. Liv looked up with surprise as recognition hit. It was the shopkeeper from the weapon supply.

Her eyes sparkled with tears, and relief filled her voice. "It's you!"

The shopkeeper, spotting Liv, ran over and knelt next to her. "Oh no! Yer hurt bad, miss!"

Heavy tears made dirty paths down Liv's cheeks. "My legs are trapped; they may be shattered. I can't really feel them anymore." She pointed behind her to the rock.

The shopkeeper's red eyes widened. "Alrigh', miss, I'm gonna have ta pull it off, and it ain't gonna feel good." He looked bleak.

Liv couldn't have felt more elated to hear that sandpaper voice again. "I know. It's okay. Just do it."

He lowered his head and walked over to the stone. "I'm gonna lift it, and when this here stone is up, you need to pull yerself forward, alrigh'?"

Liv nodded.

"Ready?"

She squeezed her eyes shut tightly and nodded again, trying to prepare for intense pain. As the shopkeeper started working the stone, it ground her legs against the debris. He grimaced as Liv let out screams as the feeling returned to her legs, but he kept going.

Liv couldn't manage the pain. "Stop! Please stop—I can't! It's too late. Just leave me here." She let out a sob and buried her head in her arms. "Just leave me."

The shopkeeper walked back over to her head. "Miss?" He tapped her arm, and Liv raised her head, her face now muddy. "Miss, we gotta try. I know it hurts, but you can't give up. I ain't leavin' ya."

Her chin quivered. "It hurts too much; my legs are crushed. I'm a stupid girl. I've compromised everything. I deserve to be here."

"We have to keep tryin'. I can get it off ya. Just be ready to pull yerself when I do." He repositioned himself near the boulder. "Ready?"

Liv took a few quick breaths in and out, starting to cry again, anticipating the searing pain that was coming.

"Miss, it's alrigh'. You can do this."

He strained as hard as he could. Liv could hear him grunt and his teeth grind together as he tried to move the boulder. Liv's screams echoed through the remaining walls in the cell, dislodging bits of rock and dust. He managed to lift the stone high enough. "Go!" he shouted in a strained voice. "Go!"

Liv pulled herself with her arms as hard as she could; her elbows dug into sharp bits of stone that sank deep into her skin. She flinched and screwed her face up but kept pulling her body away from the stone. She let out a last loud scream and forced herself forward once more.

"Alrigh', yer clear!"

Liv heard the stone crash down again, and she dropped onto her chest, panting. Her elbows were freshly bleeding, and her legs wouldn't move.

The shopkeeper came around to face Liv. "It looks pretty bad, miss. I'm sorry."

Liv turned herself over with another loud yell, having to lift her legs with her arms. They were like socks filled with jelly.

Without warning, the shopkeeper picked her up. "Sorry, miss, but you won't be walking with those legs. They're both crushed from the knee down."

Liv grabbed fistfuls of the shopkeeper's shirt, and looked up. "I thought I would die here, and if it hadn't been for you, I would have. Thank you." She gritted her teeth but still sounded sincere.

"Don't think nothin' of it, miss. Hold on tight. I'm gonna run."

Liv put her arm around his neck and shoulders and held on for dear life. He took what was left of the tower stairs slowly. As they went by, she could see one of the guard's claws hanging under the debris. She turned her face away. Once they'd cleared the stairs, his pace picked up. The bouncing due to his limp was unbearable. Liv didn't know what species the shopkeeper was, but whatever he was, he was fast when he needed to be, limp and all. They were at the bottom of the prison in a matter of minutes.

He walked them out the front gates toward the bridge, but the Mutilatus intercepted them. Liv looked up, feeling sure she was going to die, as the horrid pig creatures rounded on them and sniffed deeply.

The shopkeeper spoke assertively. "Umaro has escaped. The watcher is dead. Ya need to secure the prison. I'll send help."

They moved aside immediately and turned to enter the great doorway. Liv looked behind her at the large dungeon closing, and hoped it was the last time she would ever see it.

Up ahead, Icarus was bounding toward them, shouting, "Magnus, you found her!"

Liv raised her head slightly, and it bobbed from the movement. She was barely conscious. "Your name is Magnus?"

He nodded. In the strange way of one gravely injured, Liv didn't know why she hadn't thought to ask before this.

Icarus reached them, panting. "I saw the tower explode! Magnus was just appearing on the shore, and I sent him in after you." He looked at the gruesome sight of Liv's decimated legs. "Oh no!" he yowled.

Liv felt warm tears impending again, upon hearing Icarus's sorrowful meow. "Everything hurts." Her voice pitched with hysteria. "How are we going to get out of here?"

"Pardon, miss, but I'm a teleporter, and so is yer cat here."

Liv was thrown. "A teleporter? Icarus?"

"I have a ship out at sea. I visit the prison once a week, dropping off supplies to Emaliat, the watcher. She's my friend. Suppose it was good luck I came today."

Liv looked down, feeling the weight of her actions. "I'm so sorry about Emaliat. She was very kind to me."

Magnus looked ahead, avoiding the subject. "Alrigh'. We need to get to me ship. I have medical supplies; we can try ta get ye fixed up. Hold on. This may feel funny."

Liv nodded to Icarus as they all disappeared from the cobblestone path. The sensation was not that different from taking a portal; it was more of a pulling and much quicker. Magnus's boots landed hard on the deck of the ship, and he rushed her to the cabin. His limp made a pronounced metal clicking sound against the wood. She could see they were way out in the middle of the ocean; there was no sign of land. "How far from Pyxis are we?"

Magnus set her down gently on the bed in the cabin. "Not too far. I sail this way so's I don't have ta go through the Harbor passage. It's a lot farther, but much safer. No real access to the prison this way, but once I'm abou' thirty miles away I can teleport to the outer gates. I have permission from Olan. You can't teleport directly in the prison." He started pulling out ointments and bandages.

"Magnus?" Liv said quietly.

"Miss?"

"You saved my life. I can't express in words how thankful I am. You're so kind and gentle; I feel privileged to have met you."

Magnus blushed, and his eyes glowed vivid red. "Weren't nothin', miss. Most humans are afraid of me. Now that's twice ye showed me kindness."

"I'm not afraid of you. You're wonderful. I'm Liv, by the way. I guess you know Icarus."

Magnus poured some liquid onto a rag. "This'll sting." He placed it on her face and started to dab.

Liv flinched and shut her eyes tightly. "Ouch!"

"I know. I'm sorry, miss, but it'll help with the swelling."

Unable to be upright any longer, Liv lay down and passed out. Magnus lifted her up and shook her shoulders. "Miss! Miss, you need to stay awake. Nasty head injury—ye could die!"

She was so tired that all she wanted to do was sleep; staying awake was unbearable. With everything in her, she sat back up. Magnus started to dab the wounds again.

She politely pushed his hand away. "Do you have a mirror?"

He looked at her warily. "I don' think—"

"It's okay," she interrupted. "I need to see." She nodded and closed her eyes

He pulled a small hand mirror from a drawer. "It's pretty bad, miss. Maybe ye don't want ta look."

Liv opened her hand and flicked her fingers toward herself. In a sharp tone, she declared, "I've done the most stupid, terrible thing. Whatever I look like, it's no more than I deserve."

Magnus apparently didn't handle intense emotions well, as he seemed at a loss for words. She nodded in appreciation as he handed her the mirror reluctantly.

A gaping gash on her right temple and another on the crown of her head still bled heavily. She had four claw marks on her left cheek, and multiple lacerations were scattered all over her face. Her right cheekbone was broken, already colored purple with bruising. Her right eye had a laceration across the cornea, and all the capillaries were burst, leaving a bloodied red eye blurrily staring back at her. Her hair was sticking up every which way, covered in dirt and blood. The wound Umaro had inflicted with the needle, hung open, with torn flesh the size of a dime. Dirt clotted the bleeding, preventing her from exsanguinating. Her makeup was thoroughly smeared and shrouded the purple bruising and muddy tear streaks. Her clothing was shredded, and dirt, blood, and wounds covered her from head to toe. Expressionless, she set the mirror down and slid it away from her. She looked up at Magnus, letting him know with her expression that he had been right.

"We are on course for Harp Isle, miss. Why don' ye try to get some rest until we get there? Just don' fall asleep!"

Liv nodded, and Magnus shut the door behind him. She could hear him talking to Icarus. She knew what was coming: the anguish of the huge disappointment from everyone, the judgment, and the anger. She didn't know what the penalty was for her actions. Would she be sent to prison? Would Wes divorce her? Would she be kicked out of Lysterium permanently and removed from her role as the One? These thoughts felt like an anvil in her gut. She wished the journey back to Harp Isle would take days or wished that maybe she hadn't survived this disaster.

She looked down at her crushed legs dangling off the bed; she had no control over them. Tears glistened in her green eyes, and then, having an epiphany, she leaned over her legs and let the tears fall on them. She waited.

The tears were not healing her. Her face still hurt. Contact with the tears should have healed everything, yet nothing changed. She was in mortal pain, and her powers seemed to be gone. She looked up, blankly staring out the cabin window. "What have I done?"

As they reached the dock to Harp Isle, Liv saw Wes flying at incredible speed toward the ship. "Here we go," she said to herself, feeling sick.

She heard Wes's frantic voice and Magnus talking. "Now, Mr. Weston, it's pretty bad. It's best I warned ye first."

Wes ran into the cabin. Upon seeing her, he slammed his eyes shut and turned away as if spun by an imaginary force, slamming his fist against the door. She lowered her head to hide her face from him. He leaned his head against the worn wooden door, his eyes still closed. He slowly turned; his expression was grave, and he looked ten years older.

Wes had always been respectable, calm, and collected, but it was clear he was unraveled. His voice personified his rage. "Umaro will pay for what she's done to you." He walked over to her and gently lifted her chin up, taking in every wound. A single tear fell from one of his icy eyes, he pulled away and slammed his fist hard on the desk, cracking it in two. Liv flinched. "She has to be punished."

Liv didn't give him a chance to finish. "I know you're furious with me, but I didn't have a choice. And now because of my stupidity, Umaro has escaped." She felt a lump growing in her throat.

Wes grimaced, and then looked calmer. "I'm furious with her. I was worried sick about you. I want to hold you, but I think I might break you."

She tried to smile, but the pain quickly wiped that away. "I think I'm already broken," she joked.

He didn't smile. He took her hand. "We have to go to Olan's. You can tell all of us everything." He pulled on her hand, but she didn't move. He faltered and looked back. "Liv? I know you're feeling a lot of emotions right now, but we need to meet with everyone." He pulled again, but she still didn't move.

She looked down at her legs. "My legs were crushed. I can't walk; I can't even feel them anymore."

With tears glossing his eyes, he clenched his jaw and balled his fists. His voice was steady but had a slight shaking behind it. "I'll be right back." He left the cabin.

Liv wrung her hands with anxiety. The physical pain was excruciating, but the emotional pain was much worse. She had hurt the people who loved her and had disappointed everyone. The blood in her mouth tasted metallic, but the taste of her own blame was bitter and biting. How could she ever face them again? She wanted to curl up and disappear. She heard Olan enter the ship and caught every word of Wes's conversation with him, even though Wes kept his voice quiet. They argued about Umaro and where she would go. Olan was livid that Liv had provided Umaro an escape. Wes became angry and told Olan to see the mess she was. Liv had never witnessed Wes so angry; he wanted Umaro to suffer, and his rage radiated all around him. He had always stood up for the righteous choice, not to harm Umaro, only to stop her, but it was clear that wasn't how he felt anymore.

Wes and Olan bickered until Coralis flew in and broke up the argument. "Why don't we include Liv in this conversation? She's already heard everything."

Wes and Olan went silent. Liv could hear footsteps coming toward the cabin. Coralis entered first and gasped, coming to a dead halt. Liv lowered her head in embarrassment; she felt like a freak on exhibit with her face and body mangled. Since Coralis stopped mid-step, Olan crashed into her, which caused him to look up in surprise. He spoke in Lysterian, since Wes had enchanted her pocket watch to translate automatically for her, Liv understood the long string of swears after he viewed her face. If looks could have killed, Olan would have been dead from the look Coralis gave him.

He cleared his throat and looked down. "Sorry."

Coralis's honey-like voice was soothing. "Are you in terrible pain, dear?"

Liv stared at her for a moment, as if to say 'obviously', "It's pretty bad, but I suppose I deserve it with how angry you all are at me." She wasn't looking to feel better; she didn't want everyone to say it was okay. She hated herself for what she had done. She had jeopardized the entirety of Lysterium, and she would have to accept the consequences. Wes wouldn't enter the cabin for a long time. Liv could hear him pacing outside and knew he was listening fixedly, while she recounted what had happened.

When she came to the part where she'd been attacked while walking away, Olan seemed a little more at ease, knowing she wasn't going to give in. When Liv finished the story, they sat in silence.

Liv sighed. "Olan, what did my blood have to do with her escape?"

He rubbed the scruff on his chin, thinking. "She used old magic. The Book of Prophecy is extremely powerful and can be used as a weapon. I don't have all the answers; I need to talk to Eljene about this. That kind of magic is better explained by her. She and Uma used to be as thick as thieves; they shared everything, and Eljene taught her a lot about alchemy and the old magic. What I *do* know is that with the Book of Prophecy, she could be unstoppable, and we need to find her. My sister's back at my home. We need to consult her."

Finally, Wes walked back into the cabin. He seemed grave and wouldn't look directly at Liv. "I'll have to carry you. Can you manage that?"

Liv nodded. Before he picked her up, he waved his hand and Nomilis mended Magnus's desk that he had split in two. Then Wes, as gently as he could, lifted her from the bed. She bit her bottom lip to keep from screaming. Wes flew them to the large winged doors of Olan's home and carried her to the great room, where Eljene and Amara were conversing. They stopped talking when Wes entered, and they studied Liv's face, which now looked a bit like hamburger meat, in stunned silence.

Typically, Amara was reserved; she never raised her voice, even when she'd been chained in Umaro's castle. This time she shouted, "My word! What did she do to you?"

To save time, Amara closed her eyes briefly and using her Nomilis delved Liv's memories. She flinched as she saw the events that had taken place at the prison. She felt how much Liv hated herself at the moment. "There's no judgment," she said kindly. "I saw everything. She cornered you. Knowing you are human and think with your emotions, she hit the one trigger you would fall for. I understand, but now we have a mess on our hands—a very large mess." She turned to Eljene, who was still a little shaken by Liv's condition. "Her tears won't heal her; she's been cursed by Umaro's spell."

Eljene muttered, mostly to herself, in disbelief, "Uma did this?"

Eljene was always quirky and unaffected; this reaction was out of character. With the exception of when Wes died, which was completely appropriate. Liv felt awful that she hadn't realized how much she meant to them, until just then. Eljene pondered for a moment and then said, "We'll have to extract her stone and make an elixir. It may not heal her completely because of the curse, but it should help her be able to walk again. I'll have to perform the procedure at my home. I don't have supplies here."

Wes was still holding Liv in his arms; she was gripping his shirt to steady herself. He still wouldn't look at her. "Eljene, you should take Olan's portal. I'll fly Liv so she doesn't have to deal with the drop and pull. We'll meet you there."

Icarus had walked into the room and brushed against Wes's leg. "I'll stay behind until you've finished the procedure."

Eljene nodded slowly. It was difficult to imagine Eljene at a loss for words, which made Liv feel worse. Wes turned and walked away, never looking back, as they disappeared through the impressive doorway.

He took them high and slow to make the trip as comfortable as possible. Since they weren't going as fast as they usually did, Liv took the opportunity to talk to him now that they were alone.

Her voice was ragged and tired. "Wes, do you think you can forgive me? You won't even look at me." Her expression would have looked sad if the swelling hadn't been so severe.

Wes looked shocked. "I'm sorry I haven't looked at you. It pains me to see you like this, and it infuriates me that Umaro did this to you. When you left, I felt dreadful. I wish you had waited for everyone so we could've made a plan." His eyes were focused on the sky ahead. "I know you did what you thought you had to, but it was so dangerous and irresponsible."

Liv looked away toward the horizon. The glittering blue was fading out of sight, and the tan desert was starting to overrun the scenery. They were almost there. She hadn't thought she could feel any worse until now. She said meekly. "I'm sorry. I couldn't just let my father die. I wanted to face her and keep everyone else safe, and out of it. This is my burden. I realized too late, that Umaro had more advantages than I thought. I couldn't imagine her ever being able to escape, let alone because of me. And the worst part is, even though they're being very gracious, everyone is disappointed in me, especially you."

Wes, at last, looked at her. "I was just so worried, and seeing you like this—it snaps something in me. I don't know how to handle it. If I had lost you—" It was clear by his face he didn't want to entertain the thought. "I just want to get you better. We can figure out this whole mess after that. Let's just get you to Eljene's."

CHAPTER 10
The Elixir, the Vision, and the Revelation

WHEN THEY ARRIVED, ELJENE WAS bent over her desk with her nose about an inch from a large, dusty book. "I'm trying to pinpoint the exact spell Umaro used with the Book of Prophecy. My opinion is that since Umaro used your blood for the spell, it has hindered your powers with a curse. It quite possibly cursed her as well. Using the book in that manner has consequences."

Sharp panic jolted Liv. "Is it permanent?"

Eljene looked up. "Well, I really don't know. I need to find the spell before I can tell you that."

Liv's breathing was becoming shallow. "Do you think it's possible to heal my legs?"

"If anything will work, it'll be your elemental stone. We'll start there. Weston, place her on the ground, and give her this." She handed him a beaker of syrupy red liquid.

He carefully set her on the ground and laid her head on a pillow that he had snapped into existence. He tilted her head up to aid her with drinking the liquid. She squirmed with discomfort. Along with the pain, the liquid was bitter and thick. "What is this?" she said, trying not to gag.

"It's going to numb you so I can remove your stone."

"I'm going to be awake for it?" Liv started thrashing her arms, fighting off the beaker.

Eljene sighed in exasperation. "I'm numbing you! If you weren't human, I wouldn't even do that. I need you conscious to make sure you don't die during extraction."

"Eljene!" Wes glared at her. "That's enough."

She gave him a halfhearted apologetic glance. "I'm just worried, all right? I need to focus, so stop asking me questions."

The potion was starting to kick in. Liv already had been unable to feel her legs, but now she couldn't feel her spine or hands. "I think it's working."

Eljene started pulling out surgical instruments, and setting up a cauldron over the fire. "Good."

Within a matter of minutes, Liv couldn't feel her body at all. Everything was numb, including her tongue, which prevented her from speaking. Her eyes were the only part she could move. As Eljene approached with a scalpel, Liv raised her eyes to Wes's face in fear, shifting them from the scalpel to Wes and back. He touched her forehead to try to soothe her while she made whimpering sounds of panic.

Eljene made the first incision down her sternum. It was a strange sensation; Liv could feel the pressure of the blade but not any pain. She couldn't wrap her head around how the stone resided in her chest without causing other organ problems. Blood flowed out of the incision.

Eljene grabbed something that made Liv start to hyperventilate. "Weston, try to calm her down. You need not be stingy with your Nomilis here. I have to crack her sternum. Her heart rate is too high."

Wes seemed to be fighting his own anxiety. "I can't. She took the potion. Nothing I do has an effect on her now!"

"Fine. Cover her eyes."

Wes put his hands over her eyes. Liv blinked rapidly and made a series of high-pitched squeaks. Her breathing was becoming unstable. "I'm so sorry, try to relax."

Blinded and paralyzed, Liv suddenly heard a series of grotesque cracks. Eljene had opened her chest and was now exploring for the stone. She looked up from her surgical site; all four tiers of her monocle glasses were down. "Weston, she's tachycardic, and could arrest. I need her stable. I'm almost to the stone. Just a few more moments, and we'll be done. Get her calm!"

Wes leaned down near Liv's ear. "I'm here. Focus on my voice. It's almost over. Try, Liv. Please try to calm down." His voice was steady and comforting. She tried to focus on him, and slowly, her breathing started to regulate. Wes kissed her cheek, and she could feel the pressure of his lips on her face. His hand still covered her eyes.

Eljene's squeaky voice announced, "Got it!"

However, as Eljene removed the stone, Liv screamed and started panting, and her heart rate jumped back up. Her body was white and drenched with perspiration.

Wes looked up and yelled at Eljene, "What did you do? Put it back!"

Liv was still screaming, and Eljene was holding the stone with bloody gloves, frozen in place, with bewilderment on her face.

"Do something, Eljene!"

Liv lost consciousness, her heart rate dropped, and she stopped breathing. Wes's voice was reaching hysterical. "She's dying!"

Eljene shook as she massaged Liv's exposed heart, while Wes gave her breaths. It wasn't working. Eljene put the stone back in Liv's chest, and her heart immediately started again. Wes and Eljene looked at each other, both panting and confused.

Eljene held her gloved hands upward. "I don't understand it; it doesn't make any sense. It must be part of the curse. I can't remove her stone without killing her." She removed her tiered monocle glasses, wiped some frizzy strands of orange hair off her forehead with the back of her wrist, and set her instruments down.

Liv was still unconscious while Eljene sutured her closed. Her vitals were still not great, and her skin was pallid.

"Weston, she's lost a lot of blood, I need to make a potion. Take her into the bedroom."

When Liv woke, it was dark. She stirred and heard the bed squeak as someone moved. Wes turned on a small lamp near the bed. "You're awake! How do you feel?" His eyes were fixed on her.

Liv groaned. "I've been better." Her throat was dry and froggy. "How long was I out?"

"Hours."

"Did it work?"

Wes moved closer to her, his face somber. "Your heart stopped when Eljene removed the stone. We had to put it back. I thought we were going to lose you." He paused for a moment. "Eljene thinks that whatever Umaro cursed you with has to do with not being able to cure you."

"So, that's it? I'll never walk again?" She closed her eyes.

Wes took her hand. "We will find a way. I promise you'll walk again."

Liv turned her head away and inhaled, letting out a small sob.

"Liv, look at me."

She couldn't.

"We'll find a way. This isn't over. Once we figure out what curse she used, Eljene will be able to come up with a solution."

Liv sighed. "I don't understand. I thought an elemental stone could cure anything."

Wes looked down. "So did I. I've never encountered something like this before. Giving you a stone is the dangerous part. Once you have one—I don't understand it either. But I think all this most likely guarantees that Umaro is injured as well."

Liv wiped her tears and saw how muddy her hand was. "I'm completely caked in blood and mud. I need to shower. Will you help me?"

Wes stood, slipped his strong arms under her, and slowly lifted; she grimaced. When they reached the bathroom, he set her down on the edge of the tub.

Liv propped herself up with her arms. "Can you get me some clothes and toiletries?" *Sometimes his Nomilis really are quite handy.* Liv thought.

Wes snapped once, and everything appeared. Liv saw the clothes laid out on the vanity: long black yoga pants, a black cotton tunic, and champagne-colored underwear. She smiled. "I appreciate the comfy clothes."

Wes gave a half smile. "I figured light fabric would be the easiest to wear."

She pulled supplies from the large tote and set them on the bathtub. Wes ran the water and let it get hot. Her mouth was coated in dirt, and tasted of metal from all the blood. She brushed her teeth carefully over the tub, and to her dismay, when she spit, there was a lot more blood than she expected.

Wes turned on the shower, and the bathroom filled with steam, which felt nice on her wounds. He carefully started to undress her. He pulled her boots off, which dumped out the dagger, compass, and map she'd stowed there. Then he gently slid her jacket off, when he removed her shirt, something fell out, and landed by her foot. She looked down, curiously, and then slowly bent and picked up a small piece of parchment with strange writing on it. She let out a gasp.

Wes turned suddenly. "What? What happened? Are you all right?"

"Hand me my jacket—quick!" She felt around in the pocket, and sure enough, the coin was there. "I must have slipped it in there before the breakout." She stared at the parchment and coin and had a flash of Umaro's voice: *A deal's a deal.* Liv looked up, startled, remembering that Umaro's long, bony fingers had slipped something in her shirt.

Wes stared at the objects. "How did you get these? I haven't seen them since the wars."

"Umaro. It's the location of my father. She said, 'A deal's a deal,' after she took my blood. I forgot with all the craziness. So, you know what it is?"

"Yes, Umaro and Eljene invented it during the wars, but they haven't been used in over two thousand years. Umaro must have made one just for this. There's a spell on the prison, so magic can't be used. The only way is the Book of Prophecy."

Liv felt a knot of excitement in her stomach. "That means she really did give me the location, and Lucian is alive!"

Wes spoke with apprehension. "Liv, I don't want you to get your hopes up. There's no telling what has happened."

"Well, go on, read it—please."

Wes's mouth turned down slightly "What if—"

Liv cut him off "Wes, please, just read it!"

He spoke the words, and as they left his mouth, as if a projector turned on, a map appeared in the bathroom in between them. It zoomed in on Pyxis and then to a smaller section in a narrowed passage. It stopped on a small speck, an island.

Wes's eyes dropped down from the map and he exhaled slowly, looking grim. "He's on the island in the Harbor. I was afraid of that."

"Are you serious? I was *just* close to where he was! That whole time, no wonder she was so smug, he was right under my nose" she said angrily.

Wes was shaking his head. "Liv, you already came from the prison, and in your state, you wouldn't survive the passage. We can't go."

Liv straightened a bit on the edge of the tub. "What? We have to go! It's my dad—"

"Liv, we don't even know if he's alive. It's not worth the risk with so little facts."

"I still have to know. It *is* worth it."

"Is it?" His voice began to rise, "You don't know what the Harbor is like." He stopped. "Listen, let's not do this right now. Let's just get you cleaned up and comfortable."

Liv couldn't argue the point. She wanted to be cleansed of her terrible mistake and rest. The hot water burned her wounds but felt good on the swelling. It took her a good thirty minutes just to wash her hair. She was thorough, and the water draining was a dark brownish-red as she got all the grime and blood off. Wes helped wash her, and seeing the full extent of her wounds clearly disturbed, and angered him. Her torso was black and blue, and the neck wound was angry and swollen. She sat on the tub floor for a long time, just letting the water wash over her like a baptism. When she was clean, he dressed her, and she carefully towel-dried her hair. She then examined her face. She could see all the lacerations better now that the dirt was gone, and the wound on her head was worse than she'd thought. Wes put a bandage on it, and she swept up her partially wet curls into a bun. She slipped her pocket watch back on, tucked it under the tunic, and placed the coin map and the parchment into the front shirt pocket. Wes carried her to the living room.

Eljene had set out a sandwich and some coffee on a tray in front of Liv's preferred chair near the fireplace. She was hunched over a book. "Oh, good, you're awake! You gave us quite the scare, young lady."

"Yeah, I heard. What do we do now?" Wes set her in the chair.

Eljene chewed on the end of her pen. "Hmm. Well, we'll have to give it a day so I can research. Sit and eat. You must be hungry."

"Thank you, Eljene." She picked up half of the sandwich. She managed to eat the half but couldn't brave the other. She was so swollen that it was painful to open her mouth wide enough, and the chewing wasn't pleasant either. She sipped the warm coffee and started to relax; all the stress had worn her out. Within a few minutes, she drifted to sleep, listening to the crackling fire and the hushed voices of Wes and Eljene in the background.

She found herself standing in an empty white space that stretched for miles in all directions.

"Hello, Sugar Pea." Said a soft southern drawl.

Startled, Liv turned, her eyes sparkling with sudden tears. "Grandma!"

Mona was standing behind her.

Liv ran and gave her a hug. "Oh, Grandma, I thought I would never see you again!" She pulled out of the embrace, and her brow furrowed in confusion. "Where are we?"

Mona smiled but said nothing.

"Grandma, how are you here?"

Mona was wearing a fitted, beaded white gown that draped past her feet onto the floor. She was done up in full makeup and big hair. Her skin was pale. She reached down the front of her dress into her cleavage and pulled a necklace out.

Liv watched with confusion as Mona spoke calmly. "You need to find it."

The necklace was old. It was a large oval locket with a silver chain and silver filigree framing a black stone. Liv stared from the locket to Mona.

"What is it?"

Mona smiled and held the locket up. "You need to find the locket."

Liv felt panic creep into her heart. "I've seen that before." She looked up, trying to think.

Something moved quickly in the distance, and Liv looked up, scared. "We need to find a way out of here."

Mona's voice became a monotone. "There is no way; the way is lost."

Liv looked at her with a start. "Grandma, come on." She held her hand out.

Mona had a glazed-over stare. "There is no way; the way is lost." Suddenly, her neck started to seep blood.

Liv ran over. "Grandma, you're bleeding!" Liv's hands were shaking violently.

The blood rushed out faster, flooding scarlet over Mona's white gown and skin. "The way is lost." She fell to the ground, her eyes open wide.

"Grandma!" Liv tried to stop the bleeding. "No—Please!" Liv was crying, and then everything went dark.

She was standing on a hill overlooking Torr. Umaro was standing next to her; she looked calm and happy. Liv staggered away from Umaro, who was holding out a hand for her.

"Come look. It's beautiful, isn't it? All this will be yours someday, how lucky. I love it here." Umaro didn't speak in her usual vicious tone; she was kind, as if they were old friends. She looked down at Liv with a genuine smile. "Come look!" She was excited.

Liv cautiously walked over to where Umaro was standing. It was a memory. Liv realized Umaro wasn't talking to her at all; she was talking to someone else from the past. Umaro's eyes lit up. She was pointing at the Blood River; the water was clear and beautiful. "Isn't it wonderful?"

Liv looked at her. To whom was Umaro being so friendly, and why was the river not made of blood, as she knew it to be? Suddenly, Liv saw something around Umaro's neck catch the sun—it was the locket, gleaming. Umaro walked down the hill toward the river, and Liv ran after her. She tried to grab the locket, but Umaro disappeared.

The river turned to blood again, and suddenly, she was violently pushed into the river and fully submerged. She found the surface and gasped, thrashing to get out. Something pulled her under. She screamed, and the salty blood flooded her mouth, nose, and eyes. Slowly, a figure emerged from the blood. Liv choked and made it to the surface again. The figure grew taller, until Liv could see it was a woman. As the blood ran down, and cleared from the woman's face, she grabbed Liv by the shoulders and yelled, "Find the locket!" Liv shrieked in terror. It was her mother, Evelyn.

Liv jerked awake and gasped. She held her throat for a moment, still feeling panic. She looked around and realized she was sitting by the fireplace. She knew she had only been asleep for a few moments, since her coffee was still steaming.

Wes rounded on her. "What happened? Are you all right! Liv?"

She studied him for a minute. "Yeah. Nightmare. It didn't seem like a dream, though."

Eljene walked over ominously. "A dream? Tell me."

"It was awful."

As she explained the dream, she thought Eljene would think it was no big deal, but she was wrong. Eljene looked frightened, even pale, and she didn't speak for a long time. Wes was also silent and looked worried.

"Eljene, it was just a dream. I've been through a lot today; it triggered something. I get nightmares a lot now. It's no big deal. Wes?" She felt riddled with confusion and a little anxiety at their reactions.

Eljene raised her eyebrows high. "I would say not, considering the last dream you had involving Umaro. I think maybe you have visions, possibly even prophecies, and they are never good. The part with Umaro by the river really happened."

Liv felt the weight of yet another responsibility that was way over her head. "Great."

Eljene walked back over to her desk and pulled out a large, ancient book. "And the locket you described—that was Umaro's."

Liv sat up straight. "What!"

Eljene was unfazed. "We will get back to that, but first, I need to explain what happened at the prison," she said, pulling her monocles from her messy hair and placing them on her face.

Liv could hear a ringing in her ears as she huffed, "That seems a little important to get back to! Especially if it was a vision and I actually need to find this thing!"

Eljene looked up at her and glared. "The now is important, girl! You can't do anything in your state, and the locket has been missing for two thousand years. It's not going anywhere!" She was irritated, holding her hands on her hips.

Liv quieted. "I'm sorry. This is a lot to process right now. You're right. Go on."

Wes sat next to Liv and absently stroked her hand. Eljene pulled open the large metal clasp on the cover of the book. She flipped to a page about three-quarters of the way through. "I haven't seen a spell of this nature since the wars. It's not pleasant. And that is also curious, considering what you just saw. Why is she moving toward the past, I wonder?" Eljene glanced up at Liv to make sure she had her full attention. "The best I can make out, is that she must have used the Raven's Cry spell, based on your description of the bird."

Liv gave Eljene a strange look. "The Raven's Cry spell? What in the world is that? And why is everything dating back to the wars? What's the connection?"

Eljene was still looking at the book; she had concern written all over her face. "You and Umaro are bound to each other because of the Book of Prophecy."

Liv's face contorted. "What!"

Eljene didn't seem to notice Liv's reaction. "Yes. I haven't read the full prophecy about the two of you, but it concerns one of you overthrowing the other. Anyway, you are bound to each other because she turned dark, the prophecy activated your bloodline once that happened. She was able to use the Raven's Cry spell with your blood because you are bound by the prophecy. The Book of Prophecy is a powerful weapon; she knew what she was doing. It seems that when she performed the spell, it cursed you—and most likely her as well. She will be temporarily weakened, which is why we haven't heard of her whereabouts and why you can't be cured yet. Something this strong will take time."

Liv was still taking in the fact that she was bound to Umaro. "Wait. What? I still don't understand how she escaped."

Eljene looked slightly annoyed at Liv's slowness in following. Wes interjected. "When a prophecy is made about two people, it binds them in fate. You were the cause of her capture, so she needed your blood to reverse it and set herself free. The Raven's Cry is a destruction spell; she used the power of the book and your blood to summon it. From what you said, it was a successful spell."

Liv gave Wes a wide-eyed nod to agree with him. "But how was she able to use the book while in prison, with all the spells surrounding her cell?"

Eljene sighed. "Anyone who is written in the book can use its power. That is why it was so dire that Umaro never get her hands on it. Do you realize what she can accomplish with it? She could do anything! You're lucky to be alive! Especially since it's your blood she needed. There's so much you don't know or understand about the past."

Liv spoke timidly. "So, what is the curse on me? Will I ever be healed?"

Eljene started reading the book again, flustered. "It looks like for both of you, all your power is temporarily suspended. The place where she cut you won't heal, and all your other injuries will take much longer to heal than normal. But you have an elemental stone, so that time frame should be a few days, not a few months." Eljene made a startled face. "And that's not the worst of it. It says here that you will share memories with the one who cast the spell until the curse is lifted."

Liv sank back in her chair. "I didn't think that things could get worse." Liv was still soaking in all the bad news, when a thought occurred to her. "Wait. So the dream I had was a combination of her memories and mine?"

"Yes. I still believe you're precognitive. I've always suspected that you and Umaro were bound to each other. Now you are temporarily sharing memories, which we may be able to use to our advantage." Eljene started pacing the living room. "For now, we need to make a plan. Umaro will be weak as long as you are, which means we may have a chance of finding her and putting a stop to whatever she has planned. You should get some rest. We'll be meeting the others back in Pyxis in a few hours. We can discuss more then."

"But what about the locket? It seemed really urgent that I find it."

Eljene stopped pacing. "The locket is something I will look into. Uma didn't say much about it, I just knew she never took it off, Amara will know much more. For now, you need to rest your body."

PART 2

The Depths of Evil

C HAPTER 11
Sisters

AMARA MOVED QUIETLY THROUGH THE rich gardens outside her home, ruminating. There was a chilled breeze in Cygnus, wafting the perfume of the flowers gently through the air. She walked to the farthest edge of the gardens, away from the great alabaster castle. Her mind was swimming with unsettled emotions. From her pocket, she removed a small sphere the size of a large marble with white smoke swirling inside of it. She often took it out when she was troubled, and held it while she thought. It had been centuries since she'd used it. Somehow, it always comforted her. It was a token of better times. She debated with herself until the pit in her stomach made the decision for her. She shook the sphere with her thumb and first finger delicately and whispered into it, "Uma?"

She waited. "Uma, I know you're injured; I need to meet with you. No guards, no weapons, no tricks—just you and me. You name the location." Nothing happened. "You used to trust me in all things. Trust me now, Sister. Please."

A small voice came from the sphere. "The old battlegrounds in one hour. No sign of anyone but you, or I'm gone."

"I'll be there. Thank you."

Amara smiled softly, closing her eyes, as tears slid down her face. It brought her hope that Umaro had kept her sphere. It was a secret from childhood that only the two of them knew. She held her head up toward the sun, soaking up its warm rays, still and peaceful. After a few minutes, she lowered her head, opened her eyes, and walked toward the portal at the opposite end of the gardens.

She arrived at the crossroads, staring absently at all the colored portals with their matching trees.

Argoth approached her carefully. "My queen," he said in his grim voice, "what's troubling you?"

Amara sighed, looking up and smiling. "My dear friend, we have been through so much in this life, but I fear there is so much more to be done. And I don't know how to do it yet."

He placed his enormous, skeletal hand on her shoulder. She looked at it, put her hand on his, and said, "The time is near, and I don't know if I can do what needs to be done. I'm uncertain that Olivia can face the very heavy task in front of her. I can't see all of the pieces yet. But I feel a terrible storm coming."

Argoth, being a reaper of sorts, was not good with emotions. He inhaled deeply. "You will know in time, my queen. You have always guided this world with your goodness and hope. There is much darkness that must come to light."

The portal took her to the burning bridge of Torr. Black ash floated all around thick and heavy, the dark buildings were crumbling, and the jasper bridge was warm from the fire that constantly burned. Amara walked to the end of the bridge and turned left, heading northwest. She walked for a long time, past the city and the dark castle, until she was in an open field. The field was yellow with dead grass scattered in patches, and rusted weapons, armor, and tents were strewn here and there. Her destination was the far end of the field, where the path tapered between vast black mountains, emitting steam. When she reached the farthest edge of the field, she stopped and waited.

"Take off your jacket."

Amara turned, not startled, and opened the three-quarter-sleeve jacket made of delicate white feathers. She slowly lowered it off her shoulders, revealing her alabaster skin and her chest tattoo. Under the jacket, she wore a low-backed, strapless sweetheart bodice, which hugged her thin frame to meet a pair of high-waisted, wide-legged trousers made of black silk. She couldn't see Umaro yet; she only heard her voice.

"And your hair—no combs. Pull it down."

Her hair was carefully wrapped in a chignon held with an ornate comb. She reached around and plucked the comb from the bun. Sheets of silky magenta hair unwound, and the curls fell down her bare back. She shook her head to show that nothing else was in her hair. Umaro came out from behind the great black mountain and walked in the center of the ravine toward Amara. She walked with perfect posture, standing at her maximum height, but she was limping slightly, and cradled her right arm with her left hand. As she approached, Amara could see that Umaro's arm was raw, oozing flesh, from a burn.

Amara spoke kindly. "I see you didn't get rid of our communication sphere. There is still a part of you in there. Remember how we used them as children?" She smiled.

Umaro gave her an icy look. "I only kept it because I thought it might prove useful at some point. What do you want?" she snapped.

"Uma, why are you doing this?"

Umaro cringed. "Don't call me that!" Her voice was threatening.

Amara waited patiently, not giving away any sign of emotion on her face.

Umaro recovered from her outburst, making her voice calm and steely again. "Is that all you wanted?"

"You've cursed yourself by using the book; you're weak and outnumbered."

Umaro laughed. "Only temporarily, Sister."

"Hasn't this gone on long enough? It's been two thousand years since he died. Da—"

Umaro cut her off. "Don't you dare say his name to me!" Her hands lit with flames.

Amara lowered her head submissively. "Forgive me. It was hard on all of us. We are your family; we lost both of you that day. Why do you insist on siding with evil? Why can't you come back?"

Umaro's eyes glowed red. She snarled, "Your pitiful pleas change nothing. I made my choice a long time ago. Once the path has been committed, it cannot be altered—remember."

"You made the wrong choice! Don't you know that? It was their side that did this to you—to us. It was *their* side that took him."

"Enough!" Umaro's face was a rictus of pure hatred. Her stance was menacing "I will rule Lysterium and see all of you suffer! It's written—I'm the chosen one! When I break the spell you placed on Ectern and get to the walls, this world and the others will be mine. I'm the only one who can open them." She angrily pointed at the black mountains behind her with her wounded arm. "Come after me, and you will die." She lowered her injured arm carefully, and with her left hand, she pulled the sphere out of her pocket and threw it at Amara.

Amara didn't flinch. The sphere landed at her feet. "You will lose, Umaro."

"Do you really think that pathetic human can stop me? You know the prophecy; you know what I'm capable of. It's already over."

Umaro threw a vanishing stone at the ground and disappeared.

Amara knelt and picked up the sphere, that now had a crack in it. Tears glistened in her magenta eyes. Despairing, she sorrowfully whispered into the still air, "You will lose."

C HAPTER 12
Memories

UMARO WAS, IN FACT, WEAK and outnumbered—but not for long. She walked the narrow passage through the black mountains to a hidden opening. Two Epoch were waiting for her return at the entrance. She slapped one of them hard and screeched in anger, "How dare she bring that up!" She wasn't speaking to anyone in particular, just venting her anger. Though feared by all others, the Epoch didn't dare move. She pointed to him. "Go gather the rest of the Epoch, and ready the armory." She snapped her fingers, and a list appeared in her hand. "I'm leaving Lysterium. Everything had better be ready when I return." The Epoch sprinted to do her bidding.

She walked down a secret underground passage, made during the wars in Torr. A small bunker resided at the end, and she had been hiding there since breaking out of prison.

Umaro sat down on an old splintered bench, perturbed, resting her forehead on her hand. She sat quietly, alone in the dark for some time. A lone tear fell down her face; she wiped it with a finger and stared at the liquid with confusion and resentment. Her hand ignited, and the tear evaporated in the flames. She closed her fist, and slammed it on the bench, extinguishing the flame. She let out a growl, swept her hand through her hair, and sighed. She leaned back against the bench and tried to regain her composure. Her mind wandered to old memories, things she hadn't let herself think of in many years. She closed her eyes as she thought back to the time that brought her overwhelming pain—the ending of the wars, two thousand years ago.

***

She held the Book of Prophecy, standing by the river of blood in Torr. She stared blankly, motionless, as tears fell in lines down her beautiful face.

Delicate fingers wrapped gently around her shoulder. "Uma?" Amara turned her around to look at her. Amara's eyes were swollen and red from crying. "The funeral pyre is ready. I don't know how this happened." Umaro's hand subconsciously searched her bare chest as Amara continued. "Or who that girl was who stole it, but I promise we will find a way to get it back."

Umaro was still in shock. She sniffed and realized there were tears on her cheeks. She felt the last of her empathy slipping away as immense grief turned to cold understanding. She looked at Amara, and her blank stare slowly changed to a furrowed brow, and narrowed eyes. She finally felt something other than sorrow, a deep unyielding anger. She shook Amara's hand off of her shoulder and withdrew. "I will find that girl and rip the beating heart from her chest, like she did mine."

"Uma, I know you're devastated and upset, but we will find it. Just come with me; we need to meet the others for the ceremony." She held her hand out for her sister, waiting.

"It doesn't matter anymore. It was holding me back from what I really am. We all knew it. You wanted me to stay good, but I can't. Not anymore. Not after losing him. The curse has finally won out." Backing away from Amara, Umaro flipped open the Book of Prophecy. She chanted what she read from the book and then dropped it, it hit the earth with a loud thud. Moments later, another book appeared in her hands.

Amara slowly moved toward Umaro and her voice shook as she stared at the book in her hands. "Uma, what did you just summon? Tell me that's not the Darkwater Book. How could you possibly have summoned it?"

The book was bound in human skin, with thick black stitching. A black emblem was branded into the skin, covering most of the front. Umaro yelled, "Don't take another step toward me! You are all to blame for this! All I've ever done is serve Lysterium and defend it with my own blood and sweat, and what do I get in return?"

"Uma, listen to me. It is a terrible tragedy, but we can move forward!", Amara cried.

"No! There is no moving on. There is no *we*—not anymore." She opened the book and found the page she had been looking for. "It's over. I hate you—all of you!" she cried. "I will have my vengeance. None of you will be able to stop me!" She backed farther away from Amara and spoke the dark language. The sky filled with gray clouds, thunder roared, and a large ball of black fog formed near them.

Amara pleaded, "Uma, what are you doing? Stop—Please! Don't follow the path our grandfather did!"

Umaro drew her sword.

Amara backed away, her eyes widened with fear. "Uma, please! This isn't the answer. You know what happened to Lesto. Don't choose this!"

Out of the fog, a massive demon emerged. He emitted a terrifying resonant growl. He resembled a minotaur with enormous horns curling upward, and resplendent tattered wings. In a voice that created a shock wave he demanded, "Who dares summon me?"

Violent wind rushed over Torr, almost knocking them over. Umaro looked up at the demon, her hair blowing wildly, and her face contorted by insanity. "I did!" she screamed. "I want the power to rule everything! I want all the worlds to bow at my feet and suffer my wrath."

The demon stepped closer and looked at the book she was holding. "How did you obtain the Darkwater Book?"

Umaro stared him down, and, raising her chin a notch, did not answer.

The demon took a second heavy step toward her, causing the ground to crack under his hooves. "Very well. My price is your soul."

Amara shouted against the wind, "Uma, no!"

The demon turned toward Amara. "Silence!" He slammed his hoof to the ground, and the shockwave knocked Amara down.

Umaro didn't break her eye contact. "Take it," she said defiantly.

The demon laughed. His laughter was a haunting, deep sound like heavy stone rubbing against the walls of a cave. "Then pledge."

Umaro raised her sword and offered a mocking salute to her sister, who was reaching toward her from the ground. Umaro then hung her neck over the book, and for a moment, she locked eyes with Amara. She offered her sister a twisted smile as she slit her own throat. "It's done."

"No!" Amara screamed hysterically, tears pouring from her eyes.

Umaro's blood ran over the book, and her body crumpled slowly to the ground. The demon breathed in shakily, as though he were receiving a hedonistic thrill. The demon bent low, and inhaled sharply, causing a silvery substance to flow from Umaro's limp body and into his nostrils. He straightened as he let out a yell of exhilaration.

Umaro's body rose into the air violently. She screamed and then dropped into a seated position where she had fallen. She sat, covered in her own blood, with her head tilted straight up towards the stormy sky. Her eyes metamorphosed into completely black orbs, and she gasped as if in pain. Then she stood. Her eyes turned back to burgundy, she glanced at Amara, there was a loud clap of thunder, and the demon, Umaro, and the Darkwater Book vanished, along with the storm.

A day later, Umaro walked down the center of a field of battle. On either side of her, were gruesome creatures bloodied with injuries from the fray. The creatures did not attack, for a meeting had been called, but they were ready for anything. A great queen, their nemesis, walked among them coolly. Her destination lay in front of her: the leader of this army, Arnasic. Her burgundy eyes glinted with a spark of fire, and revealed a glimpse of her insanity. Her pyrokinetic ability was deadly if she wanted it to be; however, Umaro lit only her hands, to display power as she approached her target.

Arnasic was not like either human or Lysterian; the Darcerion army was frighteningly different from both. He had tar black scales that seemed to ooze, showing out of his three-piece tailored suit, and glistened in the sun. He stood like a tower at over seven feet, and his gaunt, long face and hollow white eyes studied Umaro. His sibilant speech formed with a reptilian mouth, "Sssso the great queen of Torr requesssstsss an audience with me. Where'sss the trap?" A wide smile crept over his face. Every tooth was pointed and sharp, and his saliva, which was black like ink, dripped from his fangs as he spoke.

Umaro appeared unfazed by his frightful demeanor; she spoke firmly. "Darcerion will never win this war—not with you in charge. You're too unorganized and predictable."

"Isss that right?" Arnasic queried. "What do you sssuggesssst?" He leaned forward eagerly.

"I suggest you use me as an asset. I will join Darcerion."

Arnasic let out a chilling laugh. "I heard about your lossss. Ha! And jusssst how do you plan to prove your allegiance to my army?"

His mockery had Umaro seething. The fire slowly crept up her arms, making its way to her neck. "Do you think you can take something from me without consequence?" she screeched. She cackled nastily and turned to the army, pointing at all of them. "You will swear allegiance to *me* or die." She turned back to Arnasic. "But not you." she breathed. "No, you will suffer for what you took from me."

The creatures restlessly moved away from Umaro. She clasped her hands together in a double fist and slammed them into the ground in front of her, hard. A shock wave moved all around where she was standing, and the earth began to crumble into a ravine. The army fled the crevice, with some unfortunates screaming to the bottom, and only Umaro and Arnasic were left standing on higher ground.

"This should be a little more intimate." Umaro smiled maliciously.

Arnasic drew a long, bloody sword from behind the unmarked suit he wore. "You think you can overthrow me? I won't sssurrender to you."

Umaro grinned cruelly. "I'm counting on that."

He laughed again, hissing loudly. "Your hatred for me is written all over you. Why doesss a queen from Lysssterium choossse alliance with your enemy? My sssside is the one that killed him. Why turn againssst your own?"

Her eyes turned black. "I want vengeance on everyone for this—starting with you." She charged.

Arnasic swung at her, but Umaro was too quick. She slid past him, slashing deep across his back. He screeched in pain. Umaro, facing away from him, whipped her sword around and stabbed behind her, causing Arnasic's green blood to spray the ground from around the blade. She turned, and he looked at her, surprised, as if unable to comprehend what had happened. She yanked her sword free while she leapt into the air, and slashed again. This time, she removed one of his legs.

Arnasic fell to the ground. He spat blood at her and laughed. "Pain does not intimidate me."

Her black eyes narrowed with hawk like focus on him. "You don't know pain—not yet." She dug her heel into his chest and then squatted down above him. She placed her thumbs in his eyes and pushed hard. Her tongue curled up to one side of her upper lip, and she smiled as green blood splattered on her face. Arnasic's screams only gave her more pleasure. She then casually gutted and slowly decapitated him.

She stood at the edge of the ravine she had created and held Arnasic's head high in the air, toward the waiting army. Fearful shrieks spread out through the ranks. Umaro spoke loudly, and forcefully so all could hear. "I am the ruler of Darcerion now. Bow to your dark queen!"

All the creatures bowed and cheered for her in allegiance, hungry for victory over long-prevailing Lysterium, knowing they could achieve it with Umaro as their ruler.

***

Umaro leaned forward on the bench in the bunker, still thinking about her violent rise to power in Darcerion. She closed her eyes and whispered in a language that was neither human, nor Lysterian. A shrieking sound pierced the silence, and black smoke circled down the passage, making its way into the bunker. Umaro looked up, her eyes shifted black, and she opened her mouth wide as the smoke crept down her throat. After a minute, her eyes turned burgundy again, and she coughed, holding her chest. She opened her palms and looked down. Each palm had a black mark, different symbols on each, and disconcertingly wicked in appearance.

She raised her arms, her elbows bent and her forearms vertically side by side; her palms faced each other, stiffly pointed straight up. As she pushed her arms and hands together, a force seemed to want to keep them apart. The muscles in her forearms tensed as she strained to put them together. Her palms, with great effort, finally touched. Time suspended momentarily as a bright light and a shock wave burst from her palms. Umaro vanished from the passage.

C HAPTER 13
Darcerion

UMARO APPEARED ON THE OUTSKIRTS of another world. This world was barren, with penetrating heat and open stretches of sand that extended for miles. It was a wasteland with many scattered towers of jagged rocks stacked on one another, reaching high into the dark sky. Throughout the wasteland, bursts of razor-sharp, white crystals erupted from the sand at harsh angles, each the size of a building, emitting scalding steam. There was no vegetation, animals, or other signs of life, only the harsh elements. For all of the wonder and beauty that Lysterium was, this place was its equal in desolation and dereliction.

Umaro walked through the desolate land. Sand whipped wildly through the air, catching in her hair and sticking to her face. The howl of the wind was the only sound, amid the miles of vast desert. Her gown swished, dragging along the sand as she walked on, and her sinking footsteps were quickly erased by the wind. Umaro came to a vast crater, while it could have held a large city, there was only one building inside. In the center of the crater was a black metal tower so tall the top was shrouded in clouds and could not be seen. Sharp, serrated triangles, angular and menacing, layered one on top of the other, covered the tower's massive width and height.

Although the long walk was harsh and difficult, she was not weary. Her power was multiplied in Darcerion. She stopped at the lip of the crater to observe her destination: a place she had not been to in many years. The terrifying creatures, that made up her army, did not reside in this region of Darcerion, rendering it unoccupied; the tower was void of guards and movement, abandoned and forgotten. As she made her way down into the crater, vivid purple lightning struck all around the tower, making a shrieking sound as it came and went. When she reached the mangled metal doors, she pushed them open and walked in.

The tower was like a giant maze, with a series of great hidden rooms requiring strange combinations of actions to find them, dizzying stairwells, and jagged, linear architecture. Umaro knew the way through the confusing tower without effort, as she had been there many times. Her black dress hugged her body as she walked toward a round steel elevator. She pulled a lever which started a mechanism with an echoing clank. When the elevator finally arrived, it was with vicious spikes covering the doorway. They slowly spiraled down, away from the door, to allow her entry, then repeated their process before the elevator speedily glided toward the top of the tower. When she reached the top, the spikes spiraled away again, and the door opened to reveal a stairway. The stairway was compact and curved, escalating up the tight cylindrical tower. Her shoes clicked against the metal. Small wall sconces, filled with an eerie blue fire, wound around the tower every six feet or so, lighting the way up the seemingly endless stairs. Umaro never faltered, took a break, or acted tired; she held her posture erect, her jaw set. Determination and anger kept her steadfast in her purpose.

She reached the top of the tower and opened the small wooden door that led to an outside landing. A thin wooden bridge connected the main tower she was standing in, to the smallest spire of the building. It was such a terrible height that the ground below was unable to be seen; only thick fog and a frightful drop waited over the edge. Her hair blew wildly in the forceful wind that picked up, causing the tower to rock violently back and forth. Umaro walked fearlessly across the rickety bridge, still nursing her burned arm. She turned the handle of the door to the smallest tower to find it locked. She tilted her head slightly, letting her scarlet locks fall over one shoulder to her hip. Reaching to the base of her skull, she picked through her thick hair and separated out a small tightly woven braid, which held a steel key interlocked near the end. She flipped her hair back off her shoulder, holding on to the braid with the key. The key had two long parallel bodies of metal that met at the handle, creating a large oval. Where the two ends of the oval should have met, one side had an elongated, curved strand of metal similar to an upside-down *Q*. She placed the key in the lock, and the door clicked open. Umaro hid the braid back in her hair and entered.

The metal room was open, with a vaulted ceiling, a great fireplace directly across from the door, and a huge oval table filled with books and beakers containing a myriad of liquids.

A greasy, tenor voice came from a dark corner as Umaro shut the door behind her. "It has been a long time since you've come to Darcerion my queen."

Umaro was wearing a red elbow-length fur shrug. She removed it, and set it on the table, revealing her blistered arm, speaking in a steady but threatening tone. "When I sent for your counsel in my prison break, you said the Book of Prophecy would free me without consequence. So why is it that my powers are limited, I'm weak, and my arm is scorched?" She slammed her good hand on the table, knocking over some of the beakers.

From the shadows, a cloaked creature emerged, cautiously. "My queen, forgive me. I cannot fully decipher Lysterium's Book of Prophecy. It shouldn't have caused a problem. But you are free now."

"And cursed!" Umaro shouted, causing the creature to flinch. "You are the prophet of Darcerion, are you not? You should have foreseen this!" Her eyes narrowed.

He cowered. "The Iron City prophets are too powerful. They put spells on the book; it has proven much more difficult to break those spells and understand it. I will try harder."

Umaro calmed. "See that you do. Now we have to figure out how to lift this curse. Start assembling an army to go back to Lysterium with me. My numbers were wiped out because of that vexing human and the royals." She made a fast flicking motion with her wrist, and the Book of Prophecy appeared in her hands. She set it on the long table. "Get to work. I want this resolved—immediately. I need my full power back to destroy the girl once and for all."

The prophet limped over to the table, opened the massive book, and began to sift through the pages. For a while, Umaro glided through the dark room, pacing, as he studied the contents of the book. Hours passed, and there was a hollow knock at the door. Umaro opened it, settling her gaze on the creature that stood on the other side.

He was a warrior, tall and lean, with bluish skin that was taut against the defined muscles and veins jutting out. His ears were pointed, and he had white eyes, cracking chapped lips, and sharp black teeth. He spoke in an unnaturally deep voice. "You summoned me? How may I serve the dark queen?"

Umaro stepped aside for the creature to enter. He did so cautiously, ducking his head to fit, and stayed near the door.

"I summoned you because I need an army assembled. I won't be staying in Darcerion long. Gather numbers, and be ready for war at my notice. I hope to leave soon. I will send word when I'm ready. You have two weeks."

The warrior nodded and lowered his head to her submissively. "I can have an army ready in one month."

Umaro had an edge to her voice. "A month is too long."

His eyes widened with fear of her wrath, but stood his ground. "It takes time, my queen. We must make weapons, and armor, and prepare the numbers needed."

"Very well. Get started."

He left quickly and without another word. Umaro closed the door, shutting out the sound of the wind.

The greasy voice emerged near the fireplace again. "My queen, I think I've found the reversal spell."

Umaro's heels clicked as she rushed across the floor. "What is it?"

The prophet pointed to a page in the book. "Here. You used the Raven's Cry spell to break free, using the blood of the human, correct?"

"Yes," Umaro said impatiently.

"In the reversal section, it reads, 'The Raven's Cry is a destruction spell which will curse the one it's performed on. In the event that it is used on someone who is bound to the other, then both parties will be cursed.'"

Umaro interrupted, furious. "Bound? Now I'm bound to that worthless human? What does that mean?"

The prophet looked up at her. "It seems your two bloodlines are bound by Lysterium's Book of Prophecy. The only way to reverse the curse is to obtain the blood of the one used to activate the spell—in this case, the human. Otherwise, you will remain hindered."

"Cryptic." She said slowly. "There isn't any other information on what that entails?"

"From what I can see, when you turned dark, the Book of Prophecy activated the human's bloodline as the defender of Lysterium, your nemesis. This is what bound your fates together. But the reversal spell for the Raven's Cry is extremely complicated; it requires power beyond my skill."

"She is too heavily guarded by the royals; in my weakened state, there isn't a way to get more blood. If this spell is so complex, then we'll have to use other means to aid us." Umaro was frustrated and didn't speak for a while, entangled in deep thought. Finally, she came to a conclusion. "We may not be able to get to her, but I have a plan, and you will need to come back to Lysterium with me."

The prophet stared at her, wide-eyed. "You wish for me to enter Lysterium? My queen, I've been banished under penalty of death!"

"You'll suffer a greater penalty from me if you don't cooperate! Besides, I hold the most power, and you will be under my protection." She snapped her fingers, and a list appeared. "Assemble these items within the hour. We have work to do."

The prophet bowed. "Yes, my queen. It will be done." He left the tower.

Umaro sat down at the table and began flipping through pages, looking for her prophecy. Her knowledge of the book's abilities was limited. Only the prophets in the Iron City were fully versed on everything it could do; they had spent millennia studying it. She took notes on parchment, weaving the pieces of the prophecy and the curse together and gathering more understanding on how she and Liv were bound.

In the origins of Lysterium, a prophecy foretold of a child to be born who would be of such importance and so powerful that she would be a weapon that would shape the future. The child would have the potential to liberate all those pure of heart. However, if the child fell into darkness, all would suffer her wrath, and evil would rule all the worlds. Umaro's grandfather, King Lesto, had turned dark, becoming the cruelest king ever to rule in history. He had sought out the child of this prophecy to use for his dark purpose, taking many lives along the way. Umaro's birth had been the dawn of a new age for Lysterium; she was the child of the original prophecy. She'd rejected the curse of darkness that was cast over her bloodline and fought for the good of Lysterium for thousands of years.

The Worthington bloodline had not appeared in the Book of Prophecy until after the wars ended in Lysterium, when Umaro sold her soul to the demon. Liv, specifically, was not the original chosen one in the prophecy, but she was later named as the true champion for Lysterium, amending a terrible mistake made in the past. It was her bloodline that was meant to stop Umaro if she gave in to the curse and turned evil. The two families were intertwined until one prevailed over the other, deciding the fate of all.

In her descent to darkness, Umaro had forgotten the last verse of her prophecy. She reflected on the time frame during which Liv was written into the book. She studied for hidden meaning and a way to unbind their fates, allowing her to destroy Liv. She smiled as she hit upon a revelation.

When the Darcerion prophet returned, she was in better spirits. "Did you get the items?"

He pulled out a watch from Earth with shaking hands, reading the time. "I will have the last of the items in an hour. I can meet you at the Dunes."

"Very well. After that, I will be leaving." Her voice pitched with excitement. "I need the Darkwater Book." She stood, and replaced her red shrug as she walked toward the door.

The prophet trembled at the name. "My queen, the Darkwater Book has been missing for two thousand years. How—?"

Umaro turned from the door with a small, crooked smile. "I know how to find it."

C HAPTER 14
The Darkwater Book

As Umaro descended the dark spiral stairs, the blue flames of the wall torches made her eyes look even more sinister, and her scarlet hair appeared almost black. She had confidence in each step, determination for her goal. The prophet was meeting her soon with the retrieved items from her list, so she could seek out the malevolent book. She opened the large door to exit the tower. The wind screamed through the crack of the door as it opened, and again, sand peppered the air and collected on Umaro's skin. She headed north toward the Dunes, where they were to meet.

She saw the prophet fighting the wind as he struggled to her. When he reached her, she asked, "Do you have the items?"

"Yes, my queen." He handed her a moderately-sized burlap bag.

She opened it with anticipation and smiled when she saw he had been successful. "Well done. I go alone from here. When I return, be ready to enter Lysterium."

The prophet bowed and walked southward back toward the tower, leaving her.

It was well known throughout Lysterium that Umaro had summoned the Darkwater Book at the end of the wars, a task that everyone believed impossible. Amara, who had witnessed this event, could not grasp how her sister had accomplished it. The Darkwater Book could not be sought or found by any natural being. The Four, being supernatural, were incapable of being deceived; they were all-knowing, extremely powerful, and charged with protecting the book upon penalty of death to any who sought it. This left the question of how Umaro had summoned the book to her location in Lysterium that day and, more importantly, how she'd survived judgment and completed a spell from it.

That had, in fact, been the beginning of the end—fate's cruel catalyst in a series of events that inevitably led to the arduous struggle that intertwined Liv's and Umaro's destined paths. This action had forever changed the future of Lysterium, Darcerion, and Earth. Whatever the outcome, Umaro was set on being the victor, and ruling all the free people of the three worlds with her wickedness.

She unbuttoned her shrug and let it slide off her shoulders slowly. The black tattoos on her palms that she used to gain entry to Darcerion had, over time, become more visible. They crawled down her inner wrists, reaching past her elbows to her triceps like spilled ink on a slanted desk. The design resembled a Rorschach test—devious splatters with indecipherable patterns and paths. They'd started randomly appearing at birth. Over the years, the tattooing had spread over her body, across her chest, caressing her neck, shoulders and arms, dripping down her ribs, and extending over her back, down her hips and thighs, growing always, like a vine. They served as a kind of encyclopedia, something that mapped out her life, including her secrets, memories, experiences, and even the darkness in her that had grown. These markings were special, unique only to her. They were faint in Lysterium, perhaps something that could be missed by the common eye, but highly visible in Darcerion. The longer she stayed, the more prominently the black pigment would show.

Umaro and Amara were born of the first prince of Lysterium and a common wood nymph. In those times, it was scandalous to mix races outside of the royal descendants, which caused a lot of pain for their family. Nymphs were born with full-body tattoos, a sign of lineage and purity of the race. Amara did not have these markings, so Umaro spent her younger years researching the history of tattoos in nymph culture, and any link with Lysterian bloodlines. She discovered that her tattoos meant something much deeper than a map of her life. The markings were an intricate web of deciphering pathways to other realms and a series of events foreseen in her prophecy, meant to guide her in life. Before the wars started, she found a map on her arm to reach the realm of the dead. She spent years studying the realm, and how to get there. Many centuries later, she found there was a way to break in; only one existing spell could achieve this.

Some things were beyond the ability to control, and Umaro was destined to take the path of darkness. Those in all worlds feared the Darkwater Book. Possessing raw dark magic, it could only be wielded by demons or angels; any living being was supposed to be incapable of understanding its power, and those who sought it were killed in the searching. It was an anomaly to most that Umaro had understood and used the book. When the balance of heaven and hell shifted, the Darkwater Book contained the recipe for the beginning of the end times on Earth. It was created by Azrael, the angel of death, who bound it with the skin of the saints and the fallen, and wrote it with his own blood. It was the most dangerous book in existence, and Azrael charged the Four to guard it at all times in the realm of the dead. Anyone who dared to enter the realm would face their wrath and judgment.

The black rubber gown Umaro wore, combined with her intricate tattooing, made her seem like a watercolor painting; everything melted together. She was equal parts stunning and menacing. She examined her left forearm, tracing the black with her first finger down about halfway, until she found the spot she wanted. She whispered as a smile crept over her face, "There you are." She reached into the burlap bag and removed a broken pocket watch, the size of a quarter, a smooth silver coin, a small bird skull, and a three-inch scalpel. She placed the skull on the coin, put the watch in the beak of the skull, and then cut the specific spot on her arm with the scalpel. She held the relics cupped in her right palm and dripped her blood over them as she spoke an incantation. Red eyes appeared in the ocular cavities of the skull, and the watch began to tick quickly, the hands spinning violently around the face.

Umaro had a hungry look. "Take me to it."

Suddenly, the beak clamped down on the watch. Thousands of red, black, white, and green feathers appeared and started swirling around her like a tornado of color. Haunting voices enveloped her. *Search the worlds in their entire splendor. Search the skies and the depths below. Seek the place no man can find, where time is lost and ever dies. Only the Four know where it hides.* Umaro clenched her jaw in expectation of the agony as she and the feathers dissipated in an explosion. As the searing pain subsided, she was standing at the mouth of a vast swamp.

Two colossal hollow trees served as the gateway. They twisted together in unnatural ways, forming an arch with a small opening to enter. The moist ground sank with each footstep, making a spongy sound, leaving behind the imprint of smashed moss and mud filling slowly with water. Huge roots flanked the swamp like sea serpents, rolling in and out of the water; which gnarled and flourished in great height and numbers, creating some areas that were impenetrable.

Green mist hovered above the deep, bubbling pools of sludgy water and gave off an eerie glow that lit the monstrous place. Old willows, twisting and knotted, hunched over toward the ground, their branches dipping into the dark water. Small paths were woven through the swamp like a maze, luring victims to a watery grave. Sheets of moss draped over and around the trees like velvet curtains, shutting out any natural light. The air was still and thick with decay; it was dark and hostile, with supernatural undertones creeping behind every sound.

Umaro gazed out at the vast land, searching for the correct route. She held out her arm, and without pause, the seemingly chaotic ink started to move until it revealed a path through the marshes. She looked up and saw the same design in the swamp layout—the hidden path she needed to take. The outlines of her route seemed to burn in her retinas as she studied the winding maze. She considered her wardrobe for a moment; her floor-length gown was not practical in this place. She snapped her fingers, and she was clothed in black latex pants that hugged her hourglass frame, substantial knee-high boots with multiple brass buckles and closures, and a black lace tunic with full sleeves. Her scarlet hair was wild from the wind in Darcerion; she pulled it all to her left side. It fell over her shoulder, and she loosely braided it, letting it hang on the boat neck of her tunic.

She had often heard stories of the realm of the dead, but she had never seen it with her own eyes. She took in every detail, knowing how improbable it was to make it there. She also knew she might not make it out alive, and this was only one of four regions in the realm. She had come so far. She couldn't stop her plan now, not when it was so close. Every second spent there was like a ticking time bomb that threatened to bring about her death, for the living were meant to enter the realm of the dead. Unfortunately, she didn't know which of the Four, or their regions, held her prize.

She followed the hidden path through the marshes, checking her arm every so often to ensure she was not going astray. The sloshing and sucking of her sinking steps grew louder the farther she made her way through the maze. The muck was getting deeper, until she was submerged to her thighs, using the willows' weeping limbs to steady herself. The thickness of trees was thinning, and her surroundings were quickly becoming open swamp, with nothing ahead for miles, but the twisting path and constant muck. Trudging through the viscous mud was exhausting and quickly reminded Umaro of her mortality, drawing stark contrast to her inexhaustibility in Darcerion. She was covered in stagnant slime and muck up to her neck now, and mud streaked her face and caked her long hair. Her injuries were painful in her struggle to work her way through the maze. She was pleased with her choice of latex; the mud did not weigh her clothing down, which made it somewhat less difficult to slide forward with each time-consuming step.

She finally reached the open clearing, and the ground began to tremble. Mud packed down in the commotion, leaving a few feet of opaque water on the surface. Umaro looked around for the source. Suddenly, hundreds of leeches were rapidly swimming through the surface layer of the water toward her. Their squirming bodies made slapping noises in the water, as they swarmed like vats of jelly poured downhill. Umaro, uncertain how to handle the situation, tried to pull herself higher out of the now compacted mud. The swarm of leeches split around her and met again as they passed and started to morph into a large figure. They molded into each other, growing larger and taller, and then abruptly turned into a towering horse with a pale rider.

The Horseman and his steed were both pallid, with a sickly green hue and hollow white irises. The horse resembled a Clydesdale, massive in size, with ripped bulky muscles protruding from rotten flesh, bulging veins, and long hair from knees to hooves. He seemed to hover above the swamp; only his hooves rested under the water, as if his girth and weight defied gravity. As Umaro took in this horrid appearance, the horse made deep grunting sounds and flourished his head up and down, stomping one of his front hooves against the muddy water in a menacing manner.

Umaro craned her neck high to glimpse the Horseman who was more frightful than the beast he rode. He wore a dense plate of armor over his left shoulder, and its thick strap expanded across his chest. He was thinly framed, with not an ounce of body fat, only taut skin and protruding sinewy muscle. His face was sunken, resembling that of a corpse; his head was covered with a tattered hood the same sickly color as his skin. In his left hand, he held a bloody scythe; his right arm from the elbow down was only bones, as if the flesh had been cleanly sucked off. All of hell was behind him, transparent writhing creatures burning in blue flames.

He spoke in a piercing banshee-like whisper with drawn out words. "You dare trespass in the realm of the dead! Come and see. I am Death, the Fourth Horseman." He looked down, pointing his skeletal hand at Umaro.

Umaro was not afraid; She faced the Horseman Death, who towered over her, as if he were a common man. She spoke coolly and confidently, never breaking eye contact. "Death, I seek an audience with you to negotiate for the Darkwater Book."

He let out a chilling shriek of laughter, so disquieting it could have stolen the warmth of flowing blood. "There will be no negotiation. The Darkwater Book is forbidden to all but Azrael, my brothers, and me, only to be used when the seventh seal is broken." He picked up his reins and started to turn his horrible steed away.

Umaro was not shaken. "Horseman!" she shouted.

He stopped and set his gaze more fiercely on her.

She continued to speak concisely and sternly. "I summoned the Darkwater Book over two thousand years ago, I have the knowledge and power to wield it. I sold my soul for its power, and now I must claim it again."

The horse squealed loudly, snaking his head forward, threateningly, until hitting the end of the reins. Death turned his skeleton hand palm up, closed all of his fingers but his first, and curled it toward himself as if to call her forward. Abruptly, she began to rise out of the swamp. Thick mud and water slid off of her body, collecting at her boots and making heavy splashes as it fell back into the swamp. She was paralyzed; as powerful and villainous as Umaro was, the Horseman was a force she could not overcome. Her feet dangled above the mud as she slowly continued to rise until she was face-to-face with him. Her right arm lifted toward him, seemingly of its own volition, and swiftly turned so her palm was facing upward. He made a swiping motion in the air, and the mud that covered her arm was wiped off, revealing her blistered skin and tattoos. The Horseman's ice-cold, bony fingers gripped her forearm. She barely stifled a scream of agony at his touch, like frost burn. He gripped her harder, as if searching for something, twisting her arm unnaturally as she squirmed.

Apparently, he found what he sought. Umaro screamed in pain, as he let go of her arm suddenly, almost as if he'd been commanded to, and spoke calmly. "The Horsemen are not to interfere; your path is set. We have orders involving your prophecy. If you succeed, we will meet once more." With his left hand, he raised his scythe. "Do not enter this place again."

He slashed the air near her throat with the scythe; simultaneously, with his other skeletal hand that was open palm down, he swiftly lowered it a few inches. As suddenly as she'd been paralyzed, she went plummeting to the ground. Death let out a sinister laugh that reverberated off the water as Umaro started to sink into the depths of the mud. She flailed her arms, trying desperately to stay above the surface, but she was no match for his power. She sank deep into the mud, all the while still hearing his laugh over the sound of her thrashing. She was so deep under the muck now that it was pitch black. Mud and water filled her mouth and nose as she screamed in panic. She kicked and swam as hard as she could toward the surface but never seemed to gain any distance upward. Suddenly, and most violently, she was jolted sideways, as if something had lassoed her around the waist, and then just as suddenly she was standing near the tower in Darcerion, dry and clean. She heard the faint laugh of Death fading away in the distance, and the Darkwater Book was under her arm.

C HAPTER 15
The Gathering Dark

IN THE EARLIEST YEARS OF Lysterium, on the boundaries of Torr, there was a great volcano. When it erupted, it caused mass destruction on Torr and its neighboring region, the Ashlands. The volcano's explosion was so devastating that there was nothing left of it, and all of Torr burned for three years. The great lakes of fire formed vast walls of mountain on each side. This area was known as the Walls of Ectern, and it was the reason Torr was the burning city and the Ashlands were clouded in soot.

The first race of Lysterium, the Fire Keepers, placed a weapon inside the eternally burning mountain that could end the worlds in fire or destroy ultimate evil. It was kept behind two colossal doors that lay beyond a waterfall of lava and a sea of fire. The Fire Keepers foretold a child to be born five centuries after their extinction—a Fire Keeper herself—who would reclaim the race. They forged a key of fire, that only the one child could use, to open the doors. The one born to open the doors would be known by three signs: she would have the gift of controlling fire, have the mark of the Fire Keepers on her skin, and be able to read the ancient language written on the doors.

When Umaro turned dark, Amara set out to block the Walls of Ectern so Umaro could not enter them. She succeeded by using a powerful spell in the Book of Prophecy, nearly losing her life to perform it. Through centuries of attempts to lift the spell, Umaro discovered that only the one who cast the spell could lift it, something often found in the Book of Prophecy. For the time, the walls were safe.

Now that Umaro had retrieved the Darkwater Book, she was determined to find a way around that spell. Her Darcerion army would take time to assemble, which would allow her the focus to find a way to accomplish this. She would need an army to get into Torr. She had no doubt that Amara would put up a fight to keep the walls safe. She knew that eliminating Liv would be the first step in tearing down the royals, but she had to get her alone. She had meticulously worked to break the blood oath, escape from prison, and devise a plan to break the curse of the Raven's Cry spell. Liv was slowly becoming an exposed target, with little protection left standing in the way.

Hiding in Darcerion would give Umaro the only thing remaining that she needed: time. While the royals scrambled to make a plan, Umaro was about to unleash a storm, and finally kill Liv. She was smart and patient, and Liv would never see it coming.

PART 3

The Harbor of Lost Ships

CHAPTER 16
A Piece of the Puzzle

LIV SAT QUIETLY IN A wheelchair that Wes had fabricated for her. They had returned to Pyxis, and all the royals were gathered in the great hall, loudly voicing their opinions.

Chauncy, Wes's father, looking more tired than normal, rubbed his forehead. "How can we make a plan if we have no idea where she is? She's off the map. We can't find her!"

"We can't sit around waiting for her to make a move and give her the upper hand!" Olan interjected.

Chauncy raised his eyebrows. "Well, where exactly do you want to start then?" he retorted.

Liv sat patiently while Wes stood and joined in the spat between Chauncy and Olan. "We should start by recruiting soldiers. She's temporarily weakened; we can use that to our advantage."

Olan's cheeks turned deep red. "How do we even know she's still weak? She's able enough to slip past us and is on the run. You know she sided with Darcerion. What's to say she isn't there?"

"How do I know? Because Olivia is still weakened!" Chauncy's tone was riddled with irritation. "And if she *is* in Darcerion, we would have no way of finding her and no means to enter. That door was closed two thousand years ago."

Olan paced with frustration. "So, you want to just wait for her to gather her Darcerion army and attack?"

Chauncy stopped in his tracks to glare wide-eyed at Olan.

Olan ceased pacing and gave an apologetic look. "She's always a step ahead. How do we get the upper hand?"

Coralis put a hand on Olan's chest and stared deeply into his eyes. His shoulders loosened a fraction.

Liv had never seen anyone in Wes's family argue like this. She knew their frustration was aimed, not at one another, but at the endless possibility of where Umaro was and what she could be doing.

Liv was starting to recover from the devastating wounds she had received during Umaro's escape. The wound on her neck, as Eljene had predicted, had not healed. She subconsciously rubbed her neck from the pain. Remnants of the deeper cuts still resided on her face, but her beauty was revealed again, now that the swelling was gone. The feeling in her legs had returned, with dozens of potions that Eljene had created, her bones were healing, and she could bear weight on them. However, they were still painful, she could only stand for short intervals. Liv squirmed in her wheelchair; she felt the conversation wasn't progressing into anything useful. She thought about her dream. She tried to quiet her mind and think of what she would do if she were in Umaro's shoes. Her body relaxed, and she slipped into a kind of trance.

She stood suddenly. Her body went tense, and her eyes stared blankly. She spoke in a creepy, dark tone. "I know where it is."

Everyone stopped arguing and stared. Wes had the most shocked look of all. He touched Liv's arm. "Liv?" Her body relaxed again, causing her to crumple out of the makeshift wheelchair to the ground. "Liv!" Wes scooped her up.

Her eyes refocused as she took in the look of surprise on everyone's face. She felt embarrassed by all the attention on her. "I know what she's after."

There was total, and uproarious commotion, for several long seconds, until Eljene stepped in and explained the connection between Liv and Umaro. That seemed to provoke an overall lifting of the mood, in the once tense room.

Wes tilted Liv's chin upward and looked at her eyes as if he were a doctor examining a patient. "Are you all right?"

Liv nodded slightly. "It's a strange feeling, really, but it doesn't hurt or have any effect on me when it's over. I just sort of—well, I guess morph into her for a moment. Then I see her memories. It's weird yet familiar." Her eyes searched around the room, as if she were looking for answers about how she really felt about the visions. "I just hope she can't do the same with me, or we may be seriously screwed. But somehow, I have a feeling she hasn't figured it out yet. I'm not sure how to explain that feeling, but I trust it." Liv turned from Wes and looked at everyone. "She's weak and injured; I can say that for sure. Something happened to her when she performed the spell. She's livid about it. She's hiding someplace I haven't seen before, with the Book of Prophecy. She found something in it, and she's going after a very old book."

Amara walked over to Liv. "Did you see any details of where she was?"

Liv looked up, trying to recall. "I haven't seen any place like this in Lysterium. She's traveling."

Amara touched Liv's temple and closed her eyes, concentrating, and was able to see the vision that Liv had using her Nomilis. "Oh no!" everyone glued their attention to her. "She's in Darcerion. She has the prophet, and they're searching for the Darkwater Book!"

The entire room seemed to sharply inhale all at once. Liv was the only one who didn't take a breath. "What's the Darkwater Book?"

Amara dropped her hand. "It's the most treacherous book in existence. The worst evil imaginable resides in it. If she obtains the Darkwater Book, along with Darcerion's prophet, her powers will be limitless." She turned to Eljene and continued. "I can't decipher some of her thoughts. They're filtered through Liv's mind, making everything fuzzy, but I think she's coming back to Lysterium."

Liv focused her mind, studying the floor intensely. "Yes. She's coming back to Lysterium." She closed her eyes, trying to concentrate on the foreign thoughts in her head. She choked suddenly. Fundamentally terrified, her eyes darted at Wes.

He touched her shoulder. "What? What did you see?"

Liv fought her heightened emotions, trying to refocus. She must have seen wrong; there had to be an error. She looked down at the floor again, her eyes darting back and forth, trying to recover the vision. Umaro's memories were controlled chaos as she sifted through them.

The room seemed to suspend with the tension of waiting. Amara had read Liv's thoughts and slid her long fingers delicately around Liv's forearm. "Liv?"

Startled, Liv pulled back, paralyzed with fear, knowing that Amara had seen what she was trying to disprove. Liv shook her head, pleading.

Olan, being of rather abrupt personality, spoke loudly. "Will someone clue the rest of us in?"

Liv turned to him, while running her eyes over everyone in the room. "She's after my father. She needs him for something."

Before anyone could speak, a blinding light filled the room, causing everyone, but Coralis, to wince and cower. The light collapsed into its source as it dimmed, and an angel was standing in the center of the room. Liv's jaw dropped, and she started to scream in pain.

Wes clapped his hands over her eyes frantically. "You can't look at him! A human will perish at the sight of an angel!"

The angel stood among them; he had four faces, his body was covered in eyes and tongues, and he had vast feathered wings that could barely fit in the room. He carried a massive silver sword encrusted with rubies and carvings in the language of Enoch.

Coralis's wide eyes were unblinking. "Azreal? What has happened?"

He turned to Coralis and spoke in a penetrating celestial voice. "Umaro has breached the realm of the dead. You must come with me now."

Without a word, they both vanished, leaving the others speechless and Liv with fresh burns around her eyes.

C HAPTER 17
The Galway Guy

ELJENE'S FINAL SET OF POTIONS had been successful; Liv could walk again, but she had a bit of a limp now. Her swelling was almost gone, and the once intense pain she'd felt was only a slight discomfort now. She and Umaro were still cursed from the spell, but Eljene's genius had found a way around part of it. Now that Liv and the others knew a portion of Umaro's plan, they prepared for the long road ahead.

After much deliberation, they decided Finn would take Liv and Wes to the Harbor by ship, to retrieve Lucian. Coralis had not returned from her meeting with Azreal, and Olan was assembling a meeting to warn the citizens of the impending danger. Chauncy and Amara would alert Argoth of what was happening and help guard the portals. Although Liv and Wes had the most dangerous task, Liv didn't want it any other way. She insisted she be the one to go to the Harbor. They had established a call for aid if things went awry that would contact Coralis immediately. Olan, an experienced sailor, had been to the Harbor many times, but, due to his royal duties, no longer often enough. Finn, however, had traveled through the Harbor countless times, making him the best choice for a guide.

At first light, Liv and Wes were preparing to meet Finn. They finished packing some supplies. The air was cold, and dark clouds wisped over the sun, leaving the sky overcast and gloomy, as if the weather empathized with the fear and anxiety Liv was feeling. She stepped outside and inhaled deeply. The salty, cold air was refreshing.

Wes followed behind her, closing the large doors to Olan's home. "Are you ready?" He looked apprehensive, and he wanted to argue the point of Liv staying behind.

Liv knew that look well, and started to walk. "Finn will be waiting." She moved to the edge of the gardens and looked out at the great expanse of Pyxis, folding her hands behind her back to hide the shaking. She had been in great danger many times since meeting Wes, and discovering Lysterium. Those experiences had been scary and, at times, life threatening; however, the prison break had been the first-time Liv really felt the weight of her mortality. She hadn't cared about dying when she saw Mona dead, or when the love of her life collapsed, or when he had bled all over her; she'd cared only about the ones she loved. This time was different. This time, she was on her own. She was brutally injured and cursed, and she felt she was to blame for what had happened. The brief things she had heard about the Harbor were terrible. She wondered if it was worse than the prison and if they would encounter Sirens, be shipwrecked, or even find Lucian at all. All these thoughts swarmed and overwhelmed her. She steadied her voice and looked up at Wes. "Are we flying?"

Wes nodded, wrapping his arms around her. To Liv's surprise, he delicately kissed her forehead, his lips lingering for a moment on her warm skin. Eljene's protection spell had made it so Wes couldn't use his special Nomilis on Liv, but his sudden kiss gave her much more, because it was real and candid. She felt herself releasing from the grip of fear and tension.

Wes sighed and lifted her with ease. They headed for the docks, where the great ship, Liv had seen once before, awaited their arrival.

As they reached the dock, the aromas of warm wood and stagnant seawater filled the surrounding area. At the end was the messy-haired Irishman, leaning against a post and finishing a cigarette while looking up at the sky.

Liv smiled at his carefree attitude. As they approached, Finn tossed his cigarette into the water and straightened up. "Didn't think I'd be seein' you so soon, little lass. You were much the worse for wear there."

Liv blushed and tucked her curls behind her ear awkwardly. "Yeah. How'd you know?"

"Magnus is my pal. Been goin' to him for years."

Liv looked down. "Oh."

Finn changed the subject. "So up for a leisurely visit to one of the most dangerous parts of Lysterium then, eh?" He leaned forward on his toes and rocked back and forth a few times while holding his suspenders, beaming. He clearly found himself hilarious. "Shall we?" He landed back on his heels and held an arm out toward the ship.

Wes looked at Liv as she snickered to herself, and the three of them boarded. The ship looked as if it had seen many rough journeys, but it was sturdy. Liv had never been on a ship before. Her imagination wandered toward being a sailor like her father, and she realized that the idea of sailing for a living held some enchantment.

Finn stood at the helm. He glanced over at Liv and raised his eyebrows up and down. She couldn't help laughing. "Are you ready for the open sea then?" he called. Wes nodded.

Finn was a one-man crew and seemed to like it that way. He was indeed slightly "off", as Olan had said, but he was entertaining and knowledgeable of the sea. Liv stood at bow and stared out at the vast blue in front of her. The wind had kicked up in their favor, and the sails flapped hard against it. Liv was beginning to understand why there were wings painted on the side of the ship; it was fast. Within what felt like minutes, they were leaving the city behind, and sailing into open water. Wes went into the cabin to look over maps and form a plan. Once the waters were steady, Finn walked down to the deck, where Liv was standing.

He leaned up against the ship, facing the helm, inches from her face, staring.

Liv looked at him sweetly. "What are you looking at?"

Finn looked her up and down with wide eyes. "Everything."

Liv turned to face Finn and crossed her arms, giving him a sassy look. "Not for your viewing pleasure! My husband is currently aboard the ship with you, and he doesn't like to share," she added triumphantly.

To her dismay, her remark didn't faze Finn. He had a sly look on his face. "So, I was thinkin' we go below deck, and I show you what a real man's like. Ya know, once you've been with an Irishman"—he caressed Liv's arm with his pinkie— "no other man can satisfy."

Liv pulled her arm away. She should have been appalled, but she found his cheesy lines and horrid crassness to be hilarious. "Oh, come on! Is that really the best line you could come up with? Not that I would ever go for you, even if I was available, which I'm not, but you would have to do better than that!"

Finn stood up straight and got closer. He pointed in the direction of the cabin. "Well, shite, what's he got that I don't? I'm much cuter, and I've got an accent." He pulled on his suspenders proudly. "Every gal loves an accent."

Liv leaned in close to Finn's face. "Well, Mr. Charming, your accent is about the only thing I do like." She turned abruptly and walked away.

Finn smiled. "Oh, I like women who play hard ta get." He whistled and stared at Liv's backside. "Love watchin' you go!" he called out.

Liv rolled her eyes and opened the door to the cabin, where Wes was. She sighed heavily.

Wes looked up from the map he was studying. "What's wrong? You're blushing."

Liv touched her cheek. "Pursuit number one," she said, gesturing with her thumb over her shoulder and shaking her head.

Wes straightened from his hunching over the map. "It's been two seconds. He's brave—I'll give him that."

"Definitely, considering you're a royal," Liv retorted jovially.

Wes extended his hand to the chair next to him. As Liv obliged, he pointed at the map. "This is where we are headed: The Harbor of Lost Ships." He pointed to another part of the map. "And this is Canary Cove, where the Sirens live."

Liv could see that they had to pass right through Canary Cove in order to get to the Harbor. Her stomach did a flip. "We have to go that close?"

Wes frowned and nodded. "It's the only passage for ships—one way in and one way out. That's why we need a guide who knows the ins and outs of the passage, and can avoid getting too close to all the threats. These waters are tricky, with much more danger than just physical. The passage is like a maze of dead ends, and only one path goes through. Many have gone mad trying to get out."

Liv swallowed. "Oh, that makes me feel loads better. Wait—if there's only one passage how do so many ships get lost?"

"It's full of narrow side paths to dead ends and ambushes. There *is* only one way in and out, but you have to know how to navigate it. That's why so many sailors get trapped. As experienced as they are, few are a match for the confusion of the Harbor. Finn used to transport prisoners in his younger days, so his experience is vital, even if he is inappropriate."

"So why is it called the Harbor of Lost Ships exactly? Other than the obvious."

Wes leaned his hands on the table and looked over at her. "Lysterium and Earth have a few portals where they intertwine with one another. There's never been an explanation as to why, but the portals weren't made by earthling or Lysterian; they've just always been. The ones unfortunate enough to happen upon these locations are rarely heard from again. The sea in Pyxis has one of the locations. Ever heard of the Bermuda Triangle? And there's one in Torr and one in my region, Elderwood. They are like black holes on Earth, and they lead to Lysterium."

Liv had not expected to hear that Elderwood had a black hole leading to it, and since she had never seen the place her husband ruled, her mind transformed it into something darker than she had originally imagined.

Wes continued, "Many sailors from Pyxis take this route back and forth unharmed, because they know the way. But if a ship traveling from Earth becomes lost, it can get sucked into the passage that leads to Lysterium, which means it immediately ends up in the Harbor passage. I suppose if I had to speculate, I'd say it was an insurance policy, if you will, to protect Lysterium from humans. If the ship manages to survive the wretched waters, rarely do the sailors. Between the Sirens, the demon, the island, and the madness, not many come out alive, and those who make it, don't know they are in another world. Everything is turned upside down."

Liv could feel trepidation rising into her throat. "Why do you say 'wretched waters'? What's it like? And wait—there's a demon?"

Wes brushed his fingers through his hair, something he often did when he was stressed. "The passage to the Harbor has incessant storms, the waves are horrendous, there are cliffs full of razor-sharp rocks, then there's the threat of the lost ships crashing against ours." He pointed to an area on the map, "There are hundreds of abandoned ships floating around here, hence the name. Many say it's haunted; others have rumored that the mad sailors wait on the Harbor island shore to attack any ships that come through. I've never had to go through it, so I'm not entirely sure what's waiting for us, and the demon is the worst part."

Liv raised her eyebrows.

"There's a very old water demon that lives in the Harbor. Many believe that's why it always storms. The demon doesn't like visitors and has been known to sink ships."

Liv put her head on the table and closed her eyes. Wes put his hand on her back and gently grazed his fingers over her absently. He'd done everything he could to avoid Liv going on this journey, and his frustration that his fears had come to pass was written on his face.

Liv groaned. "I feel sick."

Wes lifted her chin. "It's not the waters you need to worry about, love. Finn has sailed through there hundreds of times. He's one of the best sailors in Pyxis. You would have to be a little off to want to make the trip so many times. What he lacks in class, he makes up for in skill; I wouldn't sail with any other captain aside from Olan, and even he hasn't been as many times as Finn."

As if somehow on cue, Finn opened the door. He looked at Liv; her expression was still slightly ill from the news. "Oh, I see our gal told you she's leavin' you fer me, has she?" He clapped Wes on the back and continued with a cheeky tone. "Don't take it too hard, lad."

Luckily, Wes was not the jealous type. He gave Finn a bored look.

"All right, yer a decent fella. I'd be willing to share her fine arse."

Liv's jaw dropped, and Wes gave Finn a pointed look.

Liv was indignant. "Wow, do you even have a filter?"

Finn laughed heartily. "Aye, I'm only takin' a piss. Came in here to tell you we're nearing a port. This is the last chance you'll have to stop for anything. Ahead is the long haul."

Wes set his attention on Finn and seemed to go over a list in his head. "I think we have everything we need, unless there's something you need to stop for."

"Nah, I picked up e'rything I needed this morning." He walked out of the cabin, shouting as he left, "Long haul it is then!"

Liv and Wes stared at the now empty doorway, then shared a look. Liv started to laugh. "He is unbelievable."

Wes shook his head. "Well, he definitely keeps it interesting." He went back to his map.

Liv spoke slowly, stretching the last word. "Yeah, interesting."

They had sailed far out to sea now; Liv could no longer spot any land, just an endless stretch of dark water. It seemed as if hours had passed. She and Wes were sitting at the front of the ship. Liv attempted to teach him to play gin with an old pack of cards she'd found in the cabin. He commented on how strange it was that humans needed to amuse themselves all the time, but he went along with it. Finn had gone into the cabin and been there for what seemed like an hour. Liv couldn't really tell how long it had been, since she was on Lysterium time. They heard a lot of crashing around and swearing coming from the cabin, and finally, Finn emerged. He was holding a device that looked as if it belonged on Eljene—earmuffs of sorts. The apparatus had a large coil of copper as a headband, and the parts that went over the ears were a little smaller than tennis balls and filled with gears. It looked as though he had taken apart clocks and slapped them on a piece of scrap metal.

"Aha! Found 'em!" he said excitedly, holding the device high in the air.

Liv looked from him to the contraption. "What in the world is it?"

Finn puffed out his chest. "This here is my invention!" Then he pointed at Wes with a snarky tone. "I betcha he never invented anythin'!"

Liv gave Finn a cynical glare. "So—?" she said, drawing out her word.

"Aye, right. This'll keep those bloody Sirens from affecting us." He walked over to Liv and Wes. "You see this here?" He was pointing to a section that covered the ear.

"It looks like a clock." Liv said.

Finn stared at her for a minute and then went on. "After years o' study, I discovered that the Sirens register sound waves on a different level. My invention blocks out that sound wave entirely. You can hear everything around you, but their deadly song will never penetrate whilst yer wearin' these. You see, the gears are from Pyxis and Galway, my hometown. In a way, they reverse the effect of time for hearing."

Liv scrunched up her nose and narrowed her eyes at Finn. "Huh?"

"Jesus, woman, keep up!"

Liv laughed.

He continued, "It slows down only the part of time that carries the sound wave. I was always inventin' things back home, but I could ne'er have invented something like this on Earth, because it wouldn't make sense. In Lysterium, the possibilities are endless with the magic folk. That's why I didn't go back.

There're too many great things here. I love the sea; it's where I was born. But Lysterium has both magic *and* the sea."

Liv looked up at Finn. "How long have you been gone?"

Finn looked up at the sky. "I would guess forty years."

Liv gasped. "Don't you miss your family and friends? Your home and memories?" she said sentimentally.

"Nah, no family. They died when I was a boy. I do miss my hometown sometimes when I'm feelin' lonely, but it passes."

Liv looked at Wes. "Is it Lysterium that keeps him so young?" Finn didn't look a day older than thirty. She didn't think he'd come to Lysterium when he was a child.

"Yes. The aging process here is very different from that on Earth. Finn will look this age for many years, but he has to be careful; if he returns to Earth and he's too old, he'll die instantly."

Liv's eyes went huge. "What! But you don't change when you enter Earth."

Wes laughed. "That's because I was born in Lysterium. It only works that way with humans. Remember when we came back to Earth after the first visit, and your hair was suddenly longer? That was time catching up. That's why it is so vital to have a watch; if time can't find you, then you can't exist on Earth."

Liv felt devastated. She'd already known about the watch rule, but the thought hadn't occurred to her that if she were gone too long, she couldn't go home. Liv and Wes had never discussed where they would live now that they were married. Wes ruled Elderwood, if they stayed there, then she couldn't go back to earth after a certain point. Liv wrung her hands.

Wes smiled kindly. "Liv, I don't think it's anything to fret over—yet." Of all the things he could have ended with, the word *yet* was the least reassuring for Liv.

"Anyway," Finn said, interrupting, "When we get to a certain point in the Harbor, we'll have to wear these at all times. Don't take 'em off, no matter what. Yer life depends on it!" Finn handed each of them a pair and hooked his pair around one of his suspenders.

Liv had a sudden realization. "Oh—that reminds me!" She reached into her coat pocket and pulled out two corked vials. "Here." She handed a vial each to Wes and Finn.

Finn looked at it strangely. "What in the hell is this?" he said, examining the contents.

"It's my tears."

Finn, for the first time, was rendered speechless, without his usual witty retort.

Wes understood why she had given them the vials, but he gave her a worried look. "Liv, we're going to get through this. I'll protect you, and so will Finn."

"I know, but I may not be able to do the same for you. I couldn't take another session of you dying. This way, I know you'll have some sort of guarantee of aid."

Finn jumped in finally. "Hold on. What exactly am I supposed to do with this?" He held the vial up with his thumb and middle finger, confused.

Liv laughed at his expression. "My tears heal. There are so many dangers waiting for us; if you were to get mortally wounded, I want you to be safe. Pour the tears on any wound, and it will heal, even a fatal one. Wes died for me, but we discovered my tears can heal, and they brought him back to life. I just wanted to do something to help protect both of you."

Finn continued to stare with a strange expression. "Jesus, I thought you were human!" he said, alarmed.

"I am, Finn. It's just—well, the Book of Prophecy apparently chose me to be the hero of Lysterium. I have no clue why. I had to fight Umaro, and now we're on our way to intercept another one of her plots."

This was a lot of information for Finn to absorb. "Jesus, Mary, and Joseph! Kick me while I'm down, why don't ya! Umaro?"

Liv smiled. "I'm sorry, Finn. I have a very heavy burden to bear."

"I'll say!" he replied with wide eyes. "So, if yer human, how is it you have powers?"

Wes cut in. "Eljene made her an elemental stone, which she survived, obviously, and it unlocked certain gifts. The tears are one of them. Another one is a great disadvantage in our situation: enhanced hearing. I hope your invention holds up."

Finn looked up at the sky and rolled his eyes. "Aye, the pressure," he said to himself. "Well, any other kicks to me bollocks?"

Liv let out a laugh. "One more."

Finn made an exasperated noise. "What? I'm yer brother? If that's true, I'm divin' in right now."

Liv curled her lip up. "Oh God, no! But we are looking for my father. In the prison, Umaro gave me a map to find him in the Harbor, but now she's after him too. I'm not sure why, but we need to find him before she does."

Finn folded his arms and put a finger on his chin. "You know anything about 'im? His name or where he's from?"

"I never met him. I don't know where he's from, but he was a sailor too. His name is Lucian. I don't know his last name," she said, reaching into the breast pocket of her coat and pulling out Mona's envelope. She handed Finn the picture of her father.

Finn stood in silence for a long time, examining the man in the picture. He looked at Liv with a grave expression. "Jesus—I know him."

CHAPTER 18
A Glimpse of the Truth

L IV HADN'T EXPECTED TO HEAR that Finn knew her father. The surprise kept her silent as her mind raced with questions.

Finn continued to study the picture for a long time. "I shoulda recognized you. After seeing Lucian again, yer the spittin' image." He looked from the picture to Liv and back.

"Is he alive?" She was afraid to hear the answer.

Finn shrugged. "Don' know. Haven't seen 'im in years."

Liv's heart was racing. "How did you know him?"

Finn handed the picture back to Liv, and leaned against the deck. He put his hands in his pockets and pulled out a cigarette. "Well, I met 'im about twenty-some years back." He lit a match and puffed. "I was just getting established as a known sailor in Lysterium, but I didn't have my own ship at the time. I met Lucian in Pyxis. He was born there."

Liv cut him off. "Wait a minute. He was born in Lysterium?"

Wes straightened his posture and spoke louder than usual. "What? If he was born in Pyxis, then Olan would know him. He may even have a record of him."

Liv was overwhelmed by the illumination. "But that means—I mean, that would make me—"

Wes finished her sentence. "Half Lysterian."

She suddenly had a kind of understanding. "In the prison, before Umaro broke out, she called me a half-breed."

Wes's cheeks flushed. "So, she knows. She probably knows your whole history at this rate. The question is, how?"

Liv was struggling to contain all the thoughts racing through her mind. She rubbed her temples with the tips of her middle fingers. "Please—Finn, go on."

He took a drag of his cigarette. "Like I was sayin', I didn't have my own ship. Lucian was an incredible sailor. He let me tag along with 'im for a few months. We went all o'er Pyxis; he showed me the ins and outs of the place. Nice fella. I remember he met a human. I even met 'er. She came to Lysterium just for a day. What a doll that one was, and Lucian had it bad for her."

The color in Liv's face drained, and she felt suffocated. "Do you remember her name?"

Finn put his hand on his chin and looked up. "E—Ellen—Eve?" he said, struggling to recall.

"Evelyn," Liv said.

Finn snapped his fingers and pointed at Liv. "That's it—Evelyn."

Liv's eyes glossed with tears. "You met my mother?" Her voice cracked.

Finn cleared his throat. Tension was not his cup of tea, and he looked uncomfortable. "Er, should we not talk about this?" he said awkwardly.

Liv looked up, startled. "No! I want to hear everything!" She practically shouted.

Finn put his hands up. "All right, all right, woman. Easy! I didn't know 'im that well. I was kind of a peon—did grunt work for 'im. I was tryin' to get my own ship, so I took whatever experience he gave me. I know their relationship was some kind o' secret. She wasn't sposed to be in Lysterium for one reason or another, but he brought her anyway, just for the day. I remember because he came by portal. He left his ship on Earth. I didn't get to sail that day—that's how I met 'er. When Lucian came to tell me we weren't traveling, she was with 'im." He took another long drag of the cigarette. "We were s'posed to sail three days from then; he said he would be back with the ship. I ne'er heard from him again. A year later, I spoke to Coralis about gettin' a ship." He looked off with a dreamy look in his eye. "Aye, that woman, the most beautiful thing I ever set my eyes on." He shook his head and looked back at Liv. "Anyway, she spoke to Olan, and then I had a ship! That's the last I heard of Lucian. I reckoned he stayed on Earth with his love. Guess I was wrong."

Liv was ashen. She wrapped her arms around herself as if to hold everything together. "I think I need to lie down for a minute. I'm not feeling well."

Wes took her hand, and they walked to the cabin. She felt as if she might burst into a thousand pieces at any moment. He sat on the bed next to her.

"I never knew my mom was in Lysterium. I mean, Grandma told me she was taken by Umaro when I was a teen, but I didn't know she came here with my dad. My dad—that's weird to say. That must have been what initiated Umaro's attack, and why she thought my mom was the one from the prophecy." Her eyes were searching but unable to focus on anything. "And Lucian—he was from Pyxis? That would mean that all this time, Olan could have known him. And—"

"You are half Lysterian." Wes finished her sentence again. "That must have been why you took the elemental stone so well, and why you had powers you didn't realize." Wes was trying to be sensitive to how Liv was feeling, but the excitement in his voice was apparent.

That piece of information had not occurred to her until now, and she felt a million questions bubbling over. "So, if I'm half and half, maybe I do have a chance to overthrow Umaro. This is crazy." She put her hand over her eyes and grimaced. "Why is everything in my life so complicated?" She sighed dramatically and then sat up quickly. "Wes, I'm so close to knowing. When we find him, it changes everything."

Wes put his arm around her waist with a worried look and started to speak, but Liv put her hand over his mouth. "I know what you're going to say. Don't. I'm not ready to face that question yet." Her eyes pleaded with him. She knew he was about to ask her what she would do if Lucian was dead.

Wes's face softened and didn't say a word when she took her hand off his mouth. Liv leaned into his chest, tangled in the web of her questions. She missed the warm blanket of comfort that Wes usually gave her.

She was about to say this, when the ship jerked suddenly and sent her flying across the bunk. "Whoa—" Her eyes were large.

Wes was already on his feet and running for the door. "Are you all right?" He looked back at Liv, who was standing up; she nodded. When Wes turned the doorknob, a violent gust blew the door open, slamming it against the cabin wall. Papers flew everywhere. Wes grabbed Liv's hand, and they ran up to the helm. "What's going on?" Wes shouted to Finn.

He shouted back over the wind, "We're close to the passage! The storm's comin'!"

The wind was so vicious that it was difficult to stay steady. Liv was afraid she might blow away. Her hair was slapping her wildly in the face, and the sea was spewing icy water everywhere; it was like being in a hurricane.

Finn was using all his strength to keep the ship steady. The veins in his arms bulged, and he gritted his teeth. With sudden panic, he shouted, "Oy! Put on yer headphones!" He pointed ahead. "Sirens!"

With difficulty, they secured the headphones from the cabin and put them on. The ship seemed to be flying with all the wind. Liv could see jagged cliffs coming into view, and menacing black clouds moved at unnatural speeds toward them. Wes ran to the helm to help Finn, and Liv ran to the front of the ship and held on to the ropes of the sails for leverage. She remembered the potion she'd gotten at Magnus's shop. She pulled it out of her pocket and swallowed the whole thing in one gulp. Deafening thunder reverberated off the rocks, purple lightning struck, and icy shards of rain poured as they sailed into a narrow passage flanked by severe cliffs.

Finn was shouting and pointing ahead, looking concerned, but Liv couldn't hear what he was saying. A massive wave hit the ship and knocked her over hard, sending her and a mass of water sliding to the center of the deck and knocking off her headphones.

Everything went silent. She could still see Finn shouting, braving the storm, as he took hit after hit from the waves. Wes was desperately trying to get the sails down and didn't see that Liv had been knocked over. She was still on the ground, watching everything as if in slow motion, and then she heard it: the most beautiful singing in existence. It drew her in. The sound was like melted chocolate oozing out of a dessert—velvety, sultry, and arousing. She slowly stood up. The storm no longer affected her. She walked toward the front of the ship, mesmerized; she had no control over her body. She was like a marionette doll in the hands of its master. Her heart beat was loud in her ears. Her eyes glazed and rolled back in ecstasy. She reached the front of the ship. Her fingers caressed the soaked wood as she stared out at the rocks ahead. The thunder crashed again, and for a moment, for Liv, everything stopped. Wes and Finn were frozen, the crashing waves halted in midair, and the rain suspended in the sky. She stepped up onto the ledge of the ship and dove into the water.

Finn frantically screamed to Wes, "She went o'er!" but Wes couldn't hear what Finn was saying. Exasperated, Finn pointed forcefully toward the empty deck and made a diving motion with his hands. Liv was gone.

"Liv!" Wes shouted. He flew with furious speed to the deck. His eyes searched the torrent sea everywhere, and then he saw her swimming toward the rocks. "Oh no—Liv!" He called and dove into the water after her. The waves were intolerable; they seemed to avoid Liv, but Wes was taking a beating. She was gaining too much of an advantage. He tried to fly out of the water, but the waves kept knocking him deep under. His headphones were lost to the sea, and the trance started to pull him.

Suddenly, a net went over him, and Finn pulled him back onto the deck. Wes fought to get back in the water. Finn grabbed Liv's headphones from the deck and slapped them on Wes's head.

Wes quickly came out of the Sirens' trance and became frantic again. "We have to go after her!"

"No, not that way! They'll kill us fer sure. We'll sail into their territory and see if she's still alive. God be with us."

Wes grabbed Finn's shirt by the chest with a rabid-dog look. "I have to go after her! They could kill her!" He started to head toward the edge of the ship.

Finn grabbed his arm. "Get ahold of yerself, man! It's not the way!"

"Then get us there now!" he said, shrugging Finn off.

Liv was approaching the cliffs of the cove and could see five Sirens waiting on the rocks in all their terrible glory, calling to her. She smiled and paddled harder and faster to reach them. They were unaffected by the storm; not a hair was out of place or moving in the wind, and not a drop of water had touched their flawlessness.

Sheets of waist length, scarlet hair framed their terrifying beauty with wild curls, and bits of diamonds sprinkled throughout their hair, with strings of silver chains hanging beautifully around the forehead and temples. Torn sheets of sheer chiffon draped over their perfect silhouettes, leaving nothing to the imagination. Over the chiffon, each wore only a small bikini bottom made of silver metal. The fabric draped out of the bikini in shreds of material, and sparkling jewels hung from the hips, fastened to the metal, hanging down to the knee. Their skin was pearlescent, like a shell, pale and glistening. Their eyes were like glittering black ink, heavily lidded in dark burgundy, with almost pointed cheekbones. Their blood red lips were voluptuous and juicy, and their faces were so sumptuous it was dreadful. Their long, bony fingers were webbed to the knuckles, and small white wings shrouded their ankles.

They oozed sensuality and seduction. As they lured Liv in, they tilted their heads back, closing their eyes and reaching out to her. Liv reached the rocks. She stretched out her hand, and the Sirens pulled her up. They gathered in a circle around her and placed Liv's hands on their breasts, kissing her neck and hands. Fangs protruded from the Sirens' mouths. They bit Liv all over, as she writhed.

Liv was a woman who enjoyed the company of men, but she was under a seducing spell and was no longer herself. The Sirens looked at each other, staring deep into one another's eyes, conversing without words.

One of them leaned down to Liv's ear and whispered, "Come. Be one of us." The potion had worked. They didn't want to kill her, but maybe this was worse.

The idea was marvelous to Liv, and she was already changing. Her body convulsed in a savage way. She screamed and contorted in strange, unnatural positions as the Sirens' venom worked its way into her blood. They stripped her clothes off, draped her in chiffon, and placed a metal chastity belt on her. They brushed her hair and put silver headbands in it, stained her lips red with her own blood, and chained her feet so she couldn't escape.

Liv's eyes, normally a vibrant green, were fading to almost white. Only a hint of pale green remained. The convulsing stopped. She stood up. She did not look human anymore, and she smiled in a sinister way at the Sirens. The venom had superseded the woman Liv used to be, and she thirsted for the blood of sailors.

CHAPTER 19
Sirens

WHEN THE STORM HAD EBBED, Wes and Finn reached Canary Cove and the entrance to the Sirens' lair. Finn whispered to Wes, "Keep lively. We're not in Kansas anymore." His eyes were searching in every direction.

It was eerily calm. The water looked like glass, with not a ripple or wave in sight. A heavy fog rolled over the ship and misted through the jagged rocks.

Wes was trying not to panic, but the grip of dread was overwhelming. He steadied himself and looked out into the fog, pointing. "That way."

Finn slowly turned the wheel. "Are you sure?"

Wes nodded. "I can feel her. It's that way."

Finn gave a strange expression. "What?"

Wes stretched his arm out and moved it down violently to indicate quiet.

Finn.

"Huh?" Finn whipped his head around, looking for the source of the voice.

Finn, come to me.

"Who said that?"

The voice was sultry and drawn out, and it echoed in the mist. Wes looked over at Finn, confused about whom he was talking to; he hadn't heard anything. Finn looked paranoid. He heard his name again. His face lost color, and he started to tremble.

The fog separated for a moment, and Finn saw her. Liv was standing on the rocks. She pulled the chiffon off her chest slowly and reached out for him.

"Finn," she said in a voice that was no longer hers. "Don't you want me, Finn?" She started touching her hair. "I need you. I'm waiting, Finn." She lay down on the rocks and closed her eyes, rubbing her hands along her ribcage.

Liv was not a true Siren; therefore, Finn's headphones were useless against her. She did not have the song of the Sirens, which enabled the spell, but her seduction was working. Finn was lured; he was walking to the edge of the ship.

Liv slowly sat up, and a wicked smile crept over her face. "Yes. Come to me, Finn."

Wes turned just in time to see Finn walking toward the edge. He flew fast and grabbed him right before he went over. "What are you doing?"

Finn struggled against Wes but was no match for his strength. He had an animalistic look in his eyes as he stared out at Liv on the rocks.

Wes saw what was capturing Finn's attention. With a horrified face, he spoke slowly. "My God."

He threw Finn down hard on the deck and placed his foot on Finn's chest. He held one hand out, palm up, and rapidly started moving the other hand over the palm in a tight circle. Black smoke started to form between his hands, and magically, a small blackbird appeared, hovering in his hand. He whispered to it and sent it flying with amazing speed. Finn broke free while Wes was distracted, and he again tried to go overboard. Wes grabbed him by the suspenders and punched him hard, square in the nose. It worked; Finn snapped out of his trance. He was bleeding badly.

Wes felt bad. He grabbed a handkerchief out of his pocket and handed it to him. "I'm sorry, Finn, but it had to be done."

Finn put his hand up, his eyes tearing horribly, and nodded. "Much appreciated. I was about ta be Siren lunch." He wiped the blood off his face and then stared at the water. "Look out, man!" he shouted.

Liv slid off the rocks and into the water. She slowly went under, unblinking, until she was submerged. No air bubbles came up. Wes and Finn feverishly searched the water for her. A hand reached up the side of the ship, pulling on the ropes, and then another and another. The ship was surrounded by Sirens. They were climbing up the side of the ship, ready to take their prey.

"Get behind me!" Wes shouted at Finn. He made a violent pushing motion in front of them, and a blast of wind forced one of the Sirens back into the water. She hissed angrily and then flew out of the water onto the deck.

"Here we go," Wes said under his breath, and the fight began.

All six Sirens, including the newly turned Liv, were on the ship, circling Wes and Finn with hungry eyes. Wes reached behind his head, and a sword appeared. He pulled it from its sheath. Finn pulled a dagger from a strap on his ankle. They would have to be completely in sync to pull this off.

Wes focused. "Go for the ankles. If they can't fly, we'll have better odds," he whispered to Finn.

"Aye."

It was a standoff for a few moments, with Wes and Finn at the ready, and the Sirens still and staring, unblinking, with those unnatural eyes.

"Now!" Wes shouted. He force-pushed a Siren down, rolled to the ground to avoid another, and swiftly lacerated the wings on the ankle of the Siren he'd knocked down. She let out a horrid screech. *One down.*

Three Sirens were backing Finn into a corner. One raised her bony hand, straightened her fingers, and slashed Finn's arm.

"Arg!" He gripped his arm tightly, bleeding heavily. The Sirens licked their lips. "Get back, you devils!" He swung his pathetic dagger back and forth to ward them off.

Wes ran over to aid him. With precision, he sliced through two Sirens. Wes managed to cut off one of their legs, and it turned to ash and crumbled. The other he wounded in the shoulder. The third backed off to help the others for a moment.

Wes ripped part of his shirt and made a tourniquet for Finn's arm. "You all right?"

Finn nodded and patted Wes on the shoulder. The Siren whose wings Wes had cut off slashed Wes in the face with blurring speed. A deep gash rested not a centimeter below his eye. His eyes watered, and blood poured down his cheek. He dodged another blow just in time to counter with his sword to her stomach. Her screech was deafening. She fell to the ground and recoiled like a snake, slithered to the edge of the ship, and slid into the water, disappearing in the depths of the sea.

Finn attacked the Siren who was missing a limb. He had her pinned to the ground, and he made a go for her heart, but another kicked him clean across the ship. He landed hard, and the fall knocked the wind out of him. He stood, quickly gasping for air. Finn heard a sound behind him but not in time. A Siren slashed his leg at the knee, knocking him to the ground. She crept up behind and wrapped her arms around his shoulders, incapacitating him. Finn writhed like a fish out of water, and with a contemptuous look, she sank her teeth deep into his neck.

"Ah!"

She tore a large chunk of flesh from him. Blood was smeared all over her mouth and chin as she smiled maliciously.

"Finn!" Wes yelled. As he ran to reach him, Finn fell to the ground. He was bleeding out from the gaping hole in his neck. Finn tried to hold his neck tightly and fight off the Siren, but he was losing consciousness. She was about to finish him. Wes flew across the ship, and in midair, he decapitated her with one stroke. Her head rolled across the deck, black blood pooled where it landed, and her body turned to ash. Wes landed and held Finn's head up. He examined the wound; an artery was lacerated, and he was pumping out blood by the pint with every heartbeat. Finn's eyes were wide, and he was convulsing, gasping, and coughing blood.

Wes put his fingers inside Finn's neck and pinched off the bleeder. "Finn, hold on! Stay awake. Just hold on!" Wes was frantic.

He looked up and searched the deck. He could see two Sirens at the other end of the ship. He reached in his pocket and pulled out the vial of tears. Finn was still gasping, calling Wes's naming weakly. Wes removed the cork with his teeth and poured the tears onto Finn's neck. A sizzling sound erupted, and the wound started to close. It healed, and Finn stopped bleeding, but he had lost a lot of blood. He was fading into unconsciousness and turning white. Wes looked up and saw the crow's nest. He picked Finn up, threw him over his shoulder, and flew. He set Finn in the crow's nest, to keep him safe from the fight he still had to continue.

"Don't die, Finn."

When Wes landed back on the deck, he was alone. There was a macabre sense all around. He searched, on high alert, for his attackers. Heavy fog rolled over the ship again. He heard the jingling of jewels against metal, and the thump of bare, wet feet against the wood. Wes readied his sword as an image emerged, and threw him off his guard. Liv was walking toward him.

Her hips swayed seductively as she moved with ease, a slight breeze tousled her hair, and she had Wes in her sights. She stared intensely into his eyes.

Wes dropped his sword. "Liv," he said desperate, "what have they done to you?"

She threw her head back and laughed. Her eyes were completely white. She fixed them on Wes again as she sauntered over to him. She slid her hands up his chest and kissed him. She then slowly moved her hands down to his pants and started to unbutton them.

He grabbed her hand forcefully. "Stop it! This isn't you." He grabbed her shoulders. "Liv, come back to me." He shook her once.

She smiled, gracefully brushed his hands off of her, and wove her fingers through his hair. She pushed his shoulders down hard so that he was on his knees. "Don't you want me, Wes?" she said, trying to bait him. "Touch me," she whispered.

Wes closed his eyes tightly and tried to focus his mind. Liv knelt down and brushed her body against his. She pushed him down so that he was on his back and straddled him.

Wes, with a cracking voice, pleaded, "Liv, stop. Please." His eyes glazed with tears, he knew she was the bait, but he couldn't hurt her, he couldn't stop it. He felt sick with grief. She rubbed her hands up his sides, spread his arms, and slowly pulled something out of her hair. She slid her hand over Wes's ribcage and thrust a dagger into his side, her lips curling into a vicious grin. The hot pain took his breath away, he gasped, squeezing his eyes up.

Two more Sirens appeared behind him. They stabbed slender blades through his arms, pinning him to the ground like a mad scientist's specimen. He gritted his teeth with a yell.

One of the Sirens looked at Liv. "Kill him."

Liv's eyes glinted with excitement as she picked up Wes's sword.

Wes lifted his head up, and looked into her white eyes. "I love you." A few tears slid over his high cheekbones, and he laid his head down on the deck in surrender, waiting for the kill. He would rather die than use the brutality he needed to escape on his wife. He knew the Sirens would use her to every advantage. He focused his mind on his memories, thousands of years' worth in mere seconds, and he saw flashes of when he'd first fallen in love with Liv many years before. He reflected on it all, his body relaxed. Liv paused for a second, as though a conflict were fighting within her. Then she raised the sword high in the air, about to make the fatal plunge. Wes closed his eyes with remorse, yet a calm washed over him, amidst his wheezing for breath through the dagger still sticking in his side. "I'm sorry. I failed you, forgive me."

Liv let out a grunt as she lowered the heavy sword, her arms were tense with muscle strain. Suddenly, a blinding white light appeared in the sky, and she missed Wes's heart, just grazing him as the sword stuck into the wood. The Sirens screamed and shielded their faces.

Wes opened his eyes and saw Coralis hovering above the ship. She swooped down, snatched one of Wes's captors by the throat, and lifted her into the air. Coralis was emanating a pure, burning white light, and her eyes were narrowed with rage as she crushed the Siren's throat. The Siren writhed in the air as Coralis's hand started to shake, screaming as white light burst from her body. Coralis let out a kind of war cry, and focused her eyes intensely, her fury resounded as the Siren caught fire. The flames were white like rays of the sun. The Siren, still screaming, exploded, sending a shower of ash into the sea. Coralis went for her second victim; she reached behind her back, in between her wings, and unveiled a scythe. The Siren ran toward the sea, but Coralis was too quick. She whipped the scythe in a circle and cut the Siren in half. The two halves crumbled to ash and blew away in the breeze.

Liv was still sitting on top of Wes. Coralis knocked her off forcefully but not fatally.

Wes shouted, "No! Don't hurt her—She's been poisoned by them."

Coralis walked over to Wes's arms and looked him straight in the eyes. "Forgive me, dear one," she said with her honey-like voice. Wes was confused; he started to ask why, when she took a deep breath and quickly ripped the swords out of his arms.

Wes yelled in pain.

She pulled him to his feet. "Can you walk?"

He nodded as he scrunched his face up while pulling the dagger from his ribs, and dropped it on the deck.

"Good. I'll tend to you in a minute." She set her gaze on Liv, walking toward her. Her wings were spread wide, but her eyes were kind. Liv hissed, quickly, she plucked Wes's sword from the wood and lunged at Coralis. Like a heavenly ballerina, Coralis gracefully twirled on her toe to avoid the blade and knocked Liv to the ground with a backhand. Again, the bright light pulsed from Coralis, blinding Liv. She walked over and knelt where Liv was lying.

Liv scratched at her eyes and screamed. Coralis grabbed her arms and held them; she was exceptionally strong. She twisted Liv's arms around her own torso and turned Liv's body so that Liv's back was facing her. She wrapped her arms around Liv tightly. "Olivia," she said in a voice that sounded ancient, deep and almost distant "find your way back to the light."

Liv struggled to break free. She was screaming, and her skin was smoking.

"Hear my voice, and come back. Follow the light." Coralis closed her eyes. Tears fell down her face and landed on Liv's forehead. When they touched Liv's skin, they burned her, leaving a red welt.

Liv screamed louder. As her flesh continued to burn, the light became brighter. Coralis inhaled deeply; it was as if she sucked all the air from the area. She fanned her wings out wide and then shoved Liv hard, away from her. As she pushed, her wings flung forward, sending a strong wind that thrust Liv across the deck, and a blinding light like a nuclear bomb flooded the entire area.

When the light faded, Coralis was panting. Wes, unstable from his injuries, had been knocked over from Coralis's wings. He was sitting on the deck, holding his bleeding side and breathing heavily. Liv was lying on the deck. As she slowly pulled herself to a sitting position, her eyes moved back and forth rapidly and turned green again. She put her hand on her head and groaned. "Oh, what happened?" Her voice was weary and she looked around at the massacre of the ship.

Chunks of ash were strewn all over the deck, and black blood, starting to coagulate, pooled around a Siren's head. Red, bloody puddles were smeared all over the ship where Finn had been attacked. Coralis was leaning against the mast, panting, and Wes was sitting, holding his side, actively bleeding.

Liv rolled over onto to her knees, stumbling to stand, her voice was meek. "Wes?"

He looked up and saw that she was human again. "Liv!" He made his way over to where she was, and took her jaw, examining her eyes. "How do you feel?

She looked at him. "About how you look—like shit."

She shivered. She looked down and saw that she was practically naked. "Oh my God, what am I wearing?" She covered her chest with her arm and hunched her torso over her legs. Wes took his shirt off, painfully, and put it around her. "What happened? Why am I dressed like this? God, if Finn sees me like this—"

Wes cut Liv off. "Oh no, Finn. Coralis, I put him in the crow's nest!" Wes tried to stand, but the stab wound to his side had punctured a lung, and he was winded and weak.

Coralis flew up to the nest, found Finn, and brought him to the deck. He was a sallow bluish pale, unconscious, and barely breathing.

Liv stared open-mouthed. "What happened? Finn!" She shook him; he didn't respond to touch.

Coralis looked up at Wes with dread, and then she shook her head, lowering her eyes. "Any moment. Azrael is coming." She looked up at the sky.

Liv looked from Coralis to Finn. "Where's his vial? Give him my tears—quick!"

Wes groaned. "I already tried that. It healed the neck wound, but his blood loss—"

"Make him drink it," Liv interrupted.

Without question, Coralis pulled the vial from Finn's pocket, opened his mouth, and poured the salty tears down his throat. Within a matter of minutes, Finn's color returned. He started coughing and sat up on his own. He grimaced as Coralis helped him stand, and she walked him to the cabin to clean his wounds.

Liv looked at Wes's wounds. "Wes, let me see." She gently touched his ribs.

Wes inhaled sharply and flinched. He coughed, and blood came pouring out of his mouth. Liv screamed. Wes wiped his mouth with the back of his wrist. "My lung is punctured." He spoke only slightly louder than a whisper, and his voice was raspy.

Liv sounded hysterical. "Where's the vial I gave you?"

"I used it on Finn."

Liv jumped up and ran to the cabin. A minute later, she emerged with her vial and poured some of it onto Wes's side and arms. Then she shoved it toward his mouth, "Drink it!"

Wes took the vial and swallowed the tears. He groaned, and then coughed, spitting a bunch of blood out of his mouth.

Liv's eyes were downturned. "How do you feel?"

Wes gave a small smile. "Perfect." His face was crusted with blood, and the deep gash on his cheek was swollen and oozing. Liv tore off a piece of the chiffon she had been draped in, soaked it with tears, and wiped the wound, it slowly closed, leaving a scar under his eye. He gripped his arms in pain, where the swords had pierced them, and poured the rest of the vial on them. His cheek, arms, and torso were caked in his own blood, while his pants had Finn's blood and a random splattering of black Siren blood all over. The glacial blue of his eyes were electric against the heavy dark circles, his hair sticking every which way, he felt awful.

They stood together. Wes picked up the Siren's head and chucked it over the side of the ship.

Liv stopped very suddenly and started to hyperventilate. "Oh my God." She took five quick breaths. "Oh my God!" She took five more breaths and started crying.

Wes ran over, but she pushed him away. His eyebrows creased and reached a hand for her, confused. Her face was contorted with grief. "Wes, I tried to stop." She gasped for air through her sobs. "I didn't have control over my own body. I was under some sort of spell." She sobbed again. "I didn't remember right away. I can't believe I tried to kill you!" She covered her face with her hands. "How can you even look at me after what I've done? And Finn!" she said through muffled hands.

Wes pulled Liv's hands off of her face and spoke gently. "Look at me." Her chin quivered as she finally looked up at him. "I love you, I'll admit that scared the hell out of me, but I know what the Sirens are capable of. I know that wasn't you."

Liv let out a loud sob.

Wes smiled. He was relieved she was back to normal. "Liv, it's all right. Just don't try to be sexy for a while, okay?" He was trying to lighten the mood for both their sake, though he was still a little rattled. Liv smiled. He teased "I don't think I could handle any more of that side of you." He pretended to fan himself; his radiant smile was breathtaking. He hadn't smiled like that in a long time, and he felt happy in that moment.

Liv pushed him slightly. "Shut up," she said, blushing. "I'm traumatized, that was horrible." She looked down at herself, wrapping Wes's ripped button-down shirt around her body. Her bare legs were bloody.

"I think it was more traumatic for me." Wes nudged her.

She nodded and brought her gaze to Wes. "True, I'm so sorry. Boy, we're a mess! You want to work a little magic on this disaster?" She gave a slight smile.

Wes snapped his fingers and stepped back to admire the Nomilis generated black cotton skinny pants, high-collared black button-down blouse, deep green herringbone vest, and ballerina flats. She swept her raven-colored hair into a messy bun so it was out of her face.

Wes had never felt happier to see Liv covered up. "No more Siren lingerie, all right?" He had cleaned himself up as well; he was no longer caked in blood, and his chiseled bare chest was now covered by a navy shirt, paired with jeans and heavy black boots. He combed his messy platinum hair back with his fingers, feeling like himself again.

Liv smiled at Wes. "Much better."

Coralis and Finn emerged from the cabin, and he too had been cleaned and changed. They all looked at one another in higher spirits, relieved they had made it through that terrible ordeal.

Finn stretched his arms and groaned. "Well, that was fun. I think I need a few minutes to get the ship in sorts before we continue."

Wes, feeling immense gratitude, gave Coralis a hug. "Thank you for getting here so quickly."

She smiled sweetly. "I'm so relieved I wasn't too late. I'll stay for the rest of the journey. I'm sure more trouble will be in our future, and if the Sirens are foolish enough to return, I'll dispatch them again."

Liv looked confused. "What do you mean? Didn't you kill the Sirens?"

Wes coughed, surprised by her comment. "You can't kill a Siren. She only harmed them enough to get them away. Their bodies will regroup and heal. Coralis is one of the most powerful beings in Lysterium; if they *could* be killed, she would have rid the Harbor of them centuries ago. She's strong enough to fend them off easily because of her half-angel blood, but not permanently, no."

Liv looked around cautiously. "So, we have to face them again?"

Coralis touched Liv's cheek. "Possibly, but I doubt it. Besides, we have much worse to face. We are close to the shore." She pointed ahead of them. "Look." She patted Liv gently and walked to the helm to aid Finn.

Liv sighed deeply. "Good news all around then," she said sarcastically.

Wes took her hand. "I tried to warn you." He smiled. "Are you all right?"

"Yes, I just need a minute to gather myself." She craned her head up at him and smiled.

He kissed her head and then walked to the sails to start mending them.

C HAPTER 20
The Harbor

THEY WERE SAILING AGAIN AFTER making repairs to the ship. Canary Cove was just a cluster of rocks in the distance now, and their path narrowed between the cliffs. The water was still; only the ripples of the ship's wake disturbed the glass-like sea.

Liv was standing at the front of the ship. Wes put his hand on her shoulder, causing her to jump.

"Sorry. Didn't mean to scare you."

Liv shrugged. "Crazy day. Made me a little jumpy, I guess."

Wes wrapped his arms around her from behind and rested his chin on her head. She felt warm and safe there in his arms, but that feeling wouldn't last. Wes pointed ahead of them. "The Harbor isn't far now. We should be nearing the lost ships and then the island shore."

Liv shuddered. Her imagination was swarming with ideas of what the shore might be like. Despite Lysterium having predominantly stunning places in it, there were some places equal in terror. Torr had been frightening, but still had beauty. The prison, however, was something Liv never could have foreseen, filled with so much fear and darkness, and the Harbor was said to be worse. What would it hold for them? She stayed in Wes's embrace, wishing that the knot in her stomach would settle and that retrieving her father would be simple.

Finn called from the helm, "Oy, Wes?" waving him up to where he was.

Wes nodded, slipping his arms away from Liv's delicate waist, and headed for the helm. Liv wrapped her arms around herself. The cold was biting as she moved to the very front of the ship, so she was at the point, leaning over to watch the wood cut through the water. A sudden bump and scrape along the ship shifted her slightly. She looked over the rail in surprise, and saw the bones of a dilapidated ship. Its sails were tattered, and mold had accumulated on the mast and fabric. Most of the wood was gone; only the timbers that made up the skeleton of the ship remained. As they coasted by, Liv looked on. Her lips parted with an inhale as she saw hundreds of ships, all in varying degrees of decay and ruin, flanking both sides of the narrowing passage. A fine green mist hovered above the water, she felt unsettled.

It was eerily silent in the Harbor, except for the water parting and the ship occasionally hitting parts of the ghost ships with a thud and a scrape, which sometimes jolted them forward. Coralis had flown up to crow's nest to keep watch. There were dangers lurking, waiting. Wes and Finn were carefully watching at the helm, and all Liv could do was wait.

She folded her hands and put her elbows on the edge of the ship, resting her chin on her wrists. She stared absently at the water; the ship was barely moving now.

Something in the water moved. Liv straightened up and concentrated on the section that caught her eye. Just an inch below the surface of the water, a giant yellow eye with a slit for a pupil was staring back at her; it blinked. Liv backed away slowly, feeling her body go numb with fear. She bumped into Wes, who had been walking over to her, and gasped, unable to speak. She turned quickly with her eyes nearly popping out of her skull.

"Liv, what's wrong? What did you see?" He looked over her to the head of the ship and then back at her.

She opened her mouth, but no words would come out; she was frozen. There was a great jolt of the ship, and it stopped moving altogether. Liv and Wes were still facing each other, as Wes tried to interpret what was wrong.

Without warning, a massive tentacle ripped through the bottom of the ship, cutting it in half. Liv went flying to the front of the ship, and Wes was thrown to the other side. She could hear everyone yelling; Finn and Wes were shouting to one another as they flanked a tentacle, and Coralis was in the sky, circling the wreckage. Large planks of wood fell all around Liv. She covered her head as the chaos rained down. The section of ship she had landed on was starting to sink. More tentacles rose out of the water. This creature was the size of ten ships; it was a sickly purplish color, with yellow spots. The tentacles wrapped around all the parts of the ship, and the beast's enormous head emerged from the depths. It was squid-like but had a gaping jaw, housing thousands of pointed teeth.

Liv finally broke from her shock, and panic took over. She gripped the remains of the ship, trying to stay above the water, but it was sinking fast. Coralis was flying above the demon; Wes and Finn were slashing at tentacles in an attempt to fight it off. The sails came crashing down, and the water was littered with planks of wood and pieces of the ship. Another tentacle came down right where Liv was. She jumped into the water. As her body plunged into the icy depths, she saw the full girth of the demon. She screamed, and bubbles and water filled her mouth as she clawed toward the surface.

Finn valiantly grabbed a sword and went for the head. "You ain't takin' my ship without a fight!" he screamed, jumping high. He got a good hit in near the eye. He plunged the sword again and again. Yellow glops of gore hung from the creature, as it let out a deep, carnal screech. Wes was flying around the other side and took a hit from a tentacle, knocking him in the water. It turned back toward Finn, who was relentless in his attack, Wes shot out of the water a little disoriented. Before anyone could do anything, the creature's jaws ripped through the section of ship Finn was holding on to and swallowed him.

"Finn!" Liv screamed. Tears poured from her soaking face as she struggled to fight the waves. Water poured into her mouth. In the midst of grief, she forgot to keep treading, and she started sinking into the depths again. The seawater burned her eyes, and her fear made it difficult to swim, but she worked her arms and kicked hard to the surface. She saw a shore and made her way to it. There was nothing she could do to help the others. She clawed her way onto the sand and pulled herself up onto the shore, choking.

Wes and Coralis fought the beast. Explosions, fire, and more horrid screeches erupted. A tentacle caught Coralis and slapped her hard into the water, creating a huge wave that washed her up onto the shore. Liv braced herself with all her might, as the wave came crashing over her. She tumbled and flailed helpless in the crash, and then pawed her way to Coralis, who was face down in the sand, and turned her over. Coralis was unconscious. Liv shook her, but she wouldn't wake. Blood was pouring out of a large gash in her head. Liv quickly wiped tears from her face and eyes and smeared them all over the wound. She couldn't tell what was seawater or tears anymore. As the tears began to work, she struggled to pull Coralis higher onto the shore. Now only Wes was left to fight the creature.

She cradled Coralis in her lap as she watched in horror. She was helpless, and Wes surely couldn't win this fight. He swirled his hands on top of each other, palms facing, a blue ball of fire was growing, he lit a tentacle, stabbed at the yellow eye, and with a deafening screech, the demon retreated under the water, extinguishing the flames, though no one knew for how long. Wes spotted the girls on the shore and flew quickly to reach them. It seemed the demon had given up for the time being. Sinking further into the deep with the wreckage of the ship, great bubbles popping at the surface with bits of debris.

Wes stumbled as he landed. He clumsily ran to Liv and crashed to his knees. "Are you all right?" He took her face in his hands, panting and looking terrified.

Liv sobbed into his hands. "Finn's dead, and Coralis is unconscious. I healed her head wound."

Wes cradled her head against his chest. His shirt was torn, black soot was smeared all over his face and arms, and bloody cuts randomly covered his body. His heavy breathing moved Liv's head, as he held his bride tightly with one arm, and gripped Coralis's arm with the other hand, as if they would be lost if he didn't hold on to them. Liv had never seen him so afraid.

She pulled her head away from him, tears still falling down her cheeks without control. "Are you hurt? I was so scared."

Wes shook his head. "I thought I'd lost both of you." He was still panting. He looked toward the water, "I think it's gone, for now."

"What was that? I've never been that terrified. When I went underwater, it was huge!"

"That was the demon that lives in the Harbor—the reason for all the ghost ships. Most don't survive the passage." He looked up. "And those who do, don't usually survive the island." He shifted his eyes to indicate for Liv to look more closely at where they washed up.

Liv hadn't noticed her surroundings with all the commotion in the water. She turned her head slowly, filled with trepidation. Now that the demon had gone, everything was calm; small waves washed over the sand, making a light slapping noise. Finn's ship had sunk out of sight now. Every part of Finn was gone, fading away in the dark water. In that moment, Liv understood what Wes had meant when he said the greatest danger was madness—the horrors, loss, brokenness, and feeling of absolute hopelessness. It wasn't difficult to see how the Harbor could break someone, and how it could trap the mind, especially for someone who didn't know Lysterium existed. True monsters inhabited Lysterium, and Liv had experienced some of the worst ones in a short time. She wondered in her grief, if part of her would stay on this island forever.

C HAPTER 21
The Lost Captain

LIV SPOKE BARELY ABOVE A whisper. "My God, what happened here?"

Wes closed his eyes and took a deep breath. "That's the madness of the Harbor. We were fortunate to survive the Harbor passage, but now that we've washed up on the island, anything could be waiting." Wes was in unfamiliar territory having never been to the island. He was highly intelligent, always controlled, and overprepared on any quest or task he set out for. Now, he was in a foreign place with only rumors and stories to go off of. He found himself feeling heavy with anxiety and despair, something he wasn't accustomed to.

Jagged cliffs near the foot of the island's shore reached miles high. The sandy shore curved ahead of them and turned toward an open piece of land filled with thick black trees. There were scavenged pieces of human remains scattered throughout the sand—some were decayed to the bone, and other pieces were still sections of gore—along with rusted weapons, pools of congealed blood, and the memory of carnage. Unnerving howls could be heard in the distance, which made the lapping waves of the sea seem more inviting.

Wes walked a few paces to investigate the island. Liv was still sitting at the shore in the wet sand with Coralis lying against her stomach and legs. Waves lightly washed over them every few moments. Her wet hair was starting to dry in frizzy, voluminous waves; her eyes were ringed in black, with streaks of mascara running down her cheeks; and her face had a film of white crystal from the sea's salt. An occasional tear slipped from her blank stare, and grief overwhelmed everything. Coralis's waist length, teal hair, caked in blood, looked like rampant seaweed as it floated just under the shallow surface. Liv cupped her hand as a wave washed up, and she used the seawater to clean the blood from the part that wasn't submerged. As Liv used the bottom of her shirt to clean the ash off of Coralis's face, she began to stir.

She sat up slowly, holding her head, and turned toward Liv, squinting. "Liv, what happened?"

"You were knocked out by a tentacle, and your head was bleeding pretty badly. I healed it."

Coralis sat quietly for a moment, as if gathering herself. She seemed to swarm with thoughts as her eyes shifted. "The ship. The demon. Where are Wes and Finn?"

Liv lowered her head, staring at the sand as it swirled and danced under the lapping waves. Exhausted and cold, she spoke in a hopeless voice. "The ship sank. Finn's gone. The demon—" she tried to swallow the lump in her throat "—swallowed him. Wes is over there." She pointed down the shore, where he was walking.

Coralis had pain written on her face. She closed her eyes and put her hand on Liv's as they sat in silence. Lysterians had a way of handling grief, but Coralis always took it harder because of her angel lineage. Her compassion and empathy could have been viewed as a magical gift; they were that strong.

Coralis sighed and began wringing her hair out. "Liv, Finn lived a long, full life. I think, as strange as it sounds, that he'd be happy with the way he died. He was an adventurer; he died facing an enormous ancient water demon, defending his passengers and ship. It was a noble and courageous thing to do."

Somehow, the thought was a comfort. Liv nodded. "I think you're right, Coralis. He would've beamed telling just that sort of story about someone else. It really is how he would've wanted it. Sirens, water demons, forbidden passages—yeah." She smiled. "That was his style."

They looked at each other, sharing a moment of mutual thankfulness for the relief in their hearts, even if it was only slight. They both stood up. Water drained from Liv's pants and made a sloshing sound as she walked higher up on the shore. Coralis looked at them both and couldn't help but give a small laugh.

"What is it?"

"We look—" She let out a louder laugh. "Well, we look like we've been shipwrecked."

"We *have* been shipwrecked!" Liv raised one eyebrow, and then started to laugh.

Their clothes were tattered and torn, and they had wild hair. Coralis still had blackened arms and chest from the fight. She raised her wings, whose grand feathers were covered with water droplets, and fluttered them abruptly. Water rained down from them. She then made a prompt motion with her arm that looked as though she were wrapping an invisible strip of fabric around herself, and just as swiftly, she was in dry clothes, her long teal hair was pulled into a thick bun, and her skin was clean and porcelain again. She made the same motion toward Liv, and Liv's face was clean of smeared makeup, and she was in new dry clothes.

Liv touched her wild hair, which was growing larger by the minute as it dried in the salty air. "Thank you for the clothes." She moved with ease, happy to be dry, in a tan fitted T-shirt and wide-legged navy linen pants. "They're very pretty," she added with a small smile.

Coralis nodded, and they headed toward Wes, who was ahead, approaching a dense canvas of black trees that remained unmoving in the wind. The air was thick with the smell of iron, wet wood, and mildew. It was warm in the sun, but the wind brought a chill that was disconcerting. With each step, Liv's feet sank deep into the wet sand, which covered her trousers almost to the knee. In the struggle, she didn't notice the bodies at first. Liv gasped as she shivered against the wind—but no longer from the cold.

Wes heard them catching up to him from behind. He pointed to the black trees. "I think Lucian might be in there. I don't know what else is on this island with us, but we probably shouldn't linger to find out. There's many rumors about this place; what's true and what's myth, I'm not certain."

Liv was looking down when the quick footsteps caught her ear too late. "Look out!" Wes shouted and swiftly threw a dagger directly to the right of her. Liv dropped to the ground as Wes slammed his body into a crazed man. They both went down.

Wes was trying to pin the man's flailing arms, while he screamed and tried to bite Wes, clattering his teeth loudly with each attempt. Saliva frothed around his mouth as if he were rabid. Wes closed his eyes tightly in resignation, and swiftly snapped the man's neck.

Liv stood up with her mouth agape, Coralis had her sword drawn looking around. Wes sat in the sand with his elbows straight, resting on his knees, his hands dangled. He swiped the sand off and brushed them through his hair, which was half black at the root with soot. He jolted around, looking behind him as a growling sound was moving closer. Wes stood quickly, a mutilated, half-dog half-man, looking creature jumped out of a bush, salivating, dirty, and covered in dry blood, it began dragging the dead body away. After that, they walked closer to the water, because they didn't know what all was on the island.

Wes felt dazed. Nothing normally seemed to faze him, but for all his strength and regality, this trip had shaken him, and for all the magic and Nomilis he had, he felt completely powerless. He was beginning to wonder if this was what mortality—something he had never known before—felt like. His inner turmoil showed as lines on his handsome face. He felt Liv's hand slip into his from behind him. He didn't turn but closed his large hand around hers, and they began to walk. Her presence comforted him, slightly.

Coralis walked behind them. "It's a three-day hike to the other side; we should head toward the thicket if that's what your instinct is telling you. If we don't find him in there, I say we travel by flight. It's safer."

Wes nodded as they trudged in the cool sand and veered to the right, heading for the higher ground, where the entrance to the black canopy was. Wes couldn't shake his melancholy feeling, he was in unfamiliar emotional territory. He had faced gruesome war and terrible loss, even great dangers, but seeing the ones he loved in peril, and being defenseless against some of those forces, had snapped something inside him. He wondered if the madness was creeping into him.

The mouth of the canopy was threatening. Liv hugged Wes's arm as they approached. The trees were as black as tar from trunk to leaves; their branches writhed and twisted in an aberrant way. When they reached the opening, Wes could feel Liv hold her breath as they entered the darkness.

Coralis drew her sword again. "There's someone in there."

Liv pulled a dagger from Wes's belt, and held it in front of her. Her elemental stone had given her the power and knowledge of how to do battle, which triggered when she faced Umaro back in her castle, she waited, ready this time. A noise came from the right of them. Wes drew his sword and wrapped his arm around Liv, ushering her farther behind him. She bent her knees and parted her feet, her hand tightly gripping the dagger and her elbow bent slightly. It was so dark they couldn't see a foot in front of them; there wasn't a lot of sunlight in the Harbor, and the trees shut out all light. Coralis began to emanate a slight glow over her entire body. She looked heavenly and pure as her large wings fluttered, and her eyes glistened against the glow.

Her voice was comforting and calm. "Lucian, my name is Coralis. I'm here to help you. This is not a trap. Please come out."

Liv whispered in a cautious tone, "How does she know it's him?"

Wes gently shushed her as he gripped his sword tighter, and concentrated on what action he would need, rather than respond to Liv's question.

There was a rustling in the trees, and a shaky voice emerged. "I have a sword—Go away!"

Wes moved forward cautiously as Liv gripped his belt, and both stared anxiously at the trees.

The light surrounding Coralis intensified into a blinding glow. She walked forward, signaling for Wes to stay, and went to where the voice was coming from. A sword suddenly thrust toward Coralis. Liv shrieked, and Wes, startled, ran forward, but Coralis quickly evaded, grabbed the sword, threw it to the ground, and motioned for Wes to move back. "Lucian, I'm not going to harm you."

"They always come to harm me."

Now that they could see, they discovered there was a fresh body near the brush.

"He said that too—before he tried to kill me."

The Nomilis of empathy came through in her voice. "We are not them, Lucian. Please show yourself." She put her hands up, dropping her sword. "See? I'm unarmed."

Wes was not happy. "Coralis!" He scolded.

She glared back at him and snapped. "Quiet!"

After a moment, they heard footsteps, and the ragged man appeared. Coralis dimmed her inner light and put her hand out toward him. He was shaking but moved forward.

She smiled. "Please come out into the open, near the sea. I will be waiting for you."

Liv looked like she wanted to protest, but Coralis led them out of the trees. When they reached the shore, Liv yelled, "Why did we leave him? The whole point was to rescue him. He probably ran away!"

Coralis gave Liv a soothing smile. "He will come. Have some faith in my abilities."

Liv sighed and started to pace, but the deep sand was exhausting, so she settled on biting her cuticles. They didn't have to wait long before he emerged from the trees.

As the daylight exposed him, they saw he was emaciated and caked in filth. He was far from what he looked like in the picture Liv had of him, but it was Lucian. His hollow cheeks were prominent, even through his beard. He grimaced in the light, shutting his dark-circled eyes, which had heavy bags under them. With each step forward, his clothes hung from his body like draped fabric on a curtain rod. The wind picked up his long gray hair, his missing leg, with a piece of wood lodged in the flesh, made him struggle through the sand.

As he moved toward Coralis, he caught a glimpse of Liv. Tears welled in his eyes, and he ran as fast as he could, tripping over the sand. "Evelyn!" His voice was desperate but filled with elation.

Liv's breath caught. When he got closer, he stopped and sank as he studied Liv, shaking his head. "My mind is playing tricks again."

Liv spoke as calmly as possible. "Lucian?"

He looked up with a startled gaze at the sound of his name, nodding slowly.

"Lucian, do you know where you are?"

He lowered his eyes. "The Harbor."

"Yes. We're here to take you home."

Lucian fell to his knees and began to cry. Liv, looking bewildered, turned to Coralis as she knelt beside him. Liv put her hand on his back, his spine jutting out under it. "I'm sorry, Lucian."

He looked up with wide, teary eyes. "I've prayed to you for so long. I thought you would never come." His hands shook uncontrollably. "Thank you for finally taking me. I've been ready to die for a long time." He closed his eyes, held his arms out to his sides as wide as they could reach, and smiled as the dim sunlight caressed his hollow face.

Liv looked at Coralis with shock. Wes moved toward them, understanding the agony Lucian was feeling.

Coralis walked over and put her hand under Lucian's chin. "Lucian, look at me." He opened his eyes, still smiling. "Lucian, I'm not here to usher you into death. We are here to *rescue* you."

His arms dropped, and he looked confused. "But you're an angel. Aren't you the angel of death? I've waited for you to come. When I saw you in the trees, I knew you finally heard me."

"Lucian, yes, I am half angel, but I'm not here to take you to Azrael. We came to rescue you. This is Liv. She found you. We need to go. I promise Liv will explain everything once we're safely out of the Harbor. You need to come with us now."

As Coralis helped Lucian up, Liv pulled Wes down to her level and whispered in his ear, "Wes, how are we going to actually get off this island? I thought you could only travel here by ship."

"You can only travel by ship to get here, but once you reach the island, there's a secret path. The royals made it in case of an emergency, like the situation we're in. The passage gets narrower as it nears the prison. There's a cave that veers to the left; it's almost impossible to see it with the naked eye and even harder to get through, but we won't be over open water."

Liv interrupted. "You aren't proposing we swim! That thing is still out there!"

"No, we'll fly along the passage until we reach the cave. Then, from the prison, we can transport back to Olan. I'll have to speak with the guard about allowing us to use the banned light transport."

He knew the prospect of going back to the prison was terrifying for her. He touched her arm gently for comfort and then left to tell Coralis the plan. She would carry Lucian, and Wes would carry Liv. The trip would be quick but still dangerous.

Liv sat in the sand. Wes, having developed some Nomilis for telepathy, could hear her thoughts. She was remembering standing at the edge of the prison and looking down the passage of water, the green mist eerily elevating the terror. He felt her fear. She supposed they'd built the prison this way so that if any prisoners escaped on foot, they would face the horrors of the Harbor and open sea with little chance of survival.

Wes came back over to Liv. "I know you're scared right now. I know I said I would protect you, and I failed, but—"

Liv touched his face, which was rough with stubble. "You didn't fail anything, we're alive aren't we? We have Lucian. We wouldn't have made it without you."

Wes couldn't escape his depression that churned inside him, and he couldn't stop thinking about everything that had just happened. "Finn is dead, the ship is gone, you almost killed me because of the Sirens, and Coralis was almost eaten by the demon. I'd say that's failing."

"Wes, we made it through. You warned me about everything, and I stubbornly rushed into it. Despite that, we succeeded."

Wes turned his head upward to feel the breeze on his face. He knew he needed to stop wallowing; they still had to make it back to Harp Isle. He cleared his throat. "Are you ready?"

"Not really."

Wes studied her face.

"Yes, I'm ready. I just am not looking forward to going back there."

"Before we go, there's one more danger of the Harbor. Didn't I tell you there were three?" he said, addressing Liv's alarmed face. "As the passage funnels toward the prison, there are creatures that produce the green mist. In concentrated doses, it causes severe confusion and disorientation. We will only come to that at the end, since we are taking the cave, but you'll need to hold your breath as we pass. I'll go as fast as I can through that part."

"This day keeps getting better."

Coralis had already flown off with Lucian when Liv and Wes finally left the forsaken island.

They reached the mouth of the cave, which looked like solid rock. As they flew, they headed straight for the wall of the cliffs and then suddenly turned left. It was an optical illusion from the sea. There it was. Small and claustrophobic, but it was there. The cave sparkled with thousands of crystals. Even underwater, the crystals glowed, lighting the ominous way. The stone was dark and covered in moss. They went slowly through the narrow passage until it opened to a large pool, where Coralis had stopped. Her light was like a beacon, bouncing off all the crystals and illuminating the entire cave.

Liv leaned in near Wes's ear. "Why did she stop?"

He didn't answer right away.

"Wes?"

"You aren't going to like it."

Liv had the familiar face of panic as she looked at Coralis, who was suspended in the air while talking to Lucian, and then back at Wes.

"We have to go under."

"The water?" Liv choked.

"It's the only way to get to the other side of the cave. We have to swim under the rocks to reach the second pool, where the exit is. You'll need to get on my back. I can swim fast, but you'll need to stay calm in order to hold your breath for the length. Coralis will light the way through."

Liv looked at the deep pool of dark water, and her eyes filled with tears. "I don't think I can do it."

"It's the only way out. We *have* to do this. Just try to go somewhere else in your mind."

"Wes, I mean it. I've never been so scared. After everything that just happened you want me to willingly go back into that water, with who knows what down there, in pitch black?"

Wes set her down on a rock. "Coralis will light the way. It will be all right."

"What if something attacks us, and we are trapped in a narrow underwater passage with no way up and no way to breathe? We'll drown!"

Coralis flew over to them. "What's wrong?"

Wes was getting anxious to leave. "She's afraid of the water. I can't use my Nomilis to alter her emotions because of the potion Eljene gave her."

Coralis looked Liv straight in the eyes. "You can do this. Get on his back, take a deep breath, and stop thinking." Something in her gaze helped Liv feel more confident. Coralis looked up at Wes and nodded. "Let's go."

Liv climbed onto Wes's back, and they dove in. He felt her nails digging into him, and he tried to go faster. Coralis made her light strong, and they speedily travelled under the water. More crystals grew along the sides of the passage, and the depth below was too far to see. Wes felt Liv's panic as they passed through the enclosed space with rock above them and no sight of the end. He tried to calm her, but she started to cough and try to breathe. Wes made a sound that was muffled, and then they burst through the water to the second pool. Liv gasped as they hit air. She slid off Wes's back and dropped to the ground.

There were two passages in the belly of the cave, one followed a stream of water, and the other was a narrow stone path. They took the path that followed water. Wes picked Liv up again, and they glided toward the passage. "We're coming to the mist soon. The air will be dense, and you won't be able to see. It will make you hallucinate. Whatever you do, don't let go of me."

They flew off fast, and as promised, the passage filled with heavy green fog. Wes pushed through. They couldn't see Coralis ahead. Liv started panting. "My skin is melting!"

Hundreds of mushrooms were growing out of the stone, the water was getting more shallow, and small caterpillar-like creatures were swarming on the water. Wes moved faster as the cave swirled and blurred, turning abruptly, until there was a faint light ahead.

Liv shrieked, "The mushrooms are growing, and those creatures are after us! Wes? Where are you?" Her grip was slipping.

"Hold on. We're almost through." He was feeling light headed as they burst through the exit into the overcast sky. There was a small stretch of the sea between them and the prison bridge. Liv was trying to wipe her hands and pushing things out of her way that weren't there. They landed on the cobblestone.

Wes splashed water in her face. "Can you hear me?"

Liv looked up. "My head is killing me. You sound far away."

Wes was relieved she was coherent again. "You're going to feel sick for a little while. It'll wear off eventually."

"Why aren't you affected?" She stumbled over her words.

"It doesn't affect me like it does humans. I feel tingling, like an extremity falling asleep, and a little dizzy."

Coralis had gone into the prison to talk about the use of light transport. Such transport was only permitted for royals and had to be proven with blood. Wes helped Liv walk, but she resisted when they reached the bridge.

"I don't want to go back there, Wes. Please don't make me."

"Liv, we have to go in. We have to use the light transport, and the light door is just inside the prison."

Liv, pulled away, swaying on her feet, her head moving slightly. "I can't face those things again—the Mutilatus." Her breathing was shallow.

Wes had to force her over his shoulder as she kicked her feet in the air. "I'm sorry—We don't have time. Just close your eyes." He flew them quickly over the bridge. When they reached the great doors, the Mutilatus weren't there. In their stead was a barrier. They could see through it, but it had a green glow and almost looked like waves. Wes walked through the barrier with ease while Liv slumped over his shoulder.

Liv tapped his waist from where she hung. "Where are the Mutilatus? What was that thing?"

"They must be out looking for Umaro. This is a temporary shield. It suspends magic, and renders anyone who passes through mortal, until they leave."

They reached the large, black door carved with hideous figures that led to the light-travel chamber and stepped onto the familiar metal floor. Coralis was wrapping her hand, after cutting it to prove she was a royal, to open the door. The jeweled knobs, representing each region, were the same as the ones in Cygnus. These grisly doors, which seemed to have no business in beautiful places, such as Cygnus or Pyxis, seemed fitting in the prison. Coralis turned the blue jewel that represented Pyxis, and after a severe jolt and dropping sensation, they were stepping into the great room at Olan's home. Liv ran to a small decorative can and threw up. Olan poured a cup of tea, clearing his throat uncomfortably, and set it near her as Wes held her hair back and readied a handkerchief.

"I'm sorry, Olan." She barely got the words out before throwing up again. Olan cleared the room so she could keep a little dignity. She sat in the closest chair she could find, used the handkerchief to clean herself up, and then took a few swigs of tea. She leaned back in the chair and covered her eyes with her right hand, groaning.

Wes knelt next to the chair. "Honestly, I'm surprised you held out as long as you did." He put his hand on her knee. "With everything we just went through, I'd say you did great."

"Not helping," Liv muttered. "I need to lie down."

Wes carried her upstairs and rubbed her pounding head; she fell asleep within minutes. Wes felt the heavy sorrow of the Harbor lifting now that he was away from it, and he began to settle into his normal demeanor again.

CHAPTER 22
Lucian's Story

A NOISE WOKE LIV, IT was nighttime, Wes wasn't in the room. The chill in the air made the fine hairs on her arms stand up. She saw a slight figure walking across the gardens from the window. She slipped on a jacket, grabbed the pictures Mona had given her off the dresser, and headed for the stairs, and out the door. Liv inhaled deeply; the smell of the salty sea and the flowers from the garden were heavy in the air. The cold penetrated her lungs, causing them to burn. Her headache was gone, and she felt better after sleeping. She followed the path that wrapped around the great ship to a veranda, where she saw him. Lucian was startled by her presence and backed away out of instinct.

Liv put her hands up and whispered, "It's just me. Can I join you?"

Lucian calmed and returned his focus to the sea. His shoulders were slumped and his mouth turned down with deep creases. His sunken eyes were partially closed, with a visible twitch to his left eye, in the faint moonlight his dark circles seemed to almost swallow his eyes altogether.

"Are you feeling any better?" she asked.

He didn't look at her. "I was damned on that island for so many years. It's hard to pick up the pieces of an old life, after living through that."

Liv looked down. "Do you want to be alone?"

He finally turned toward her, he appeared to be far away in thought. "No. I can't place it, but something about you comforts me." He touched her hand, and Liv flinched slightly at the unexpected contact.

She smiled weakly. "Lucian, I have to tell you something, but I'm not sure if it's the right time. I'm worried. You've been through so much; I don't want to cause you more pain."

"It doesn't seem like anything can affect me anymore." He said, flatly.

Liv was sidetracked by his delivery. "What happened in the Harbor? I mean, how did you get there and survive all those years?"

He looked back at the sea and sighed heavily. "I go back to that place every second of every day—what my life was before this happened, the promise of my future." The memory clearly haunted him. "My life was good. I'm from Pyxis. I became a captain early in life. When my father was alive, he started a trade with a company on Earth. My mother died during my birth, so it was just me and him. He took me with him to Earth sometimes when I was a child. I was a young man when he died. I took over the business; I had a new life to build. I have many fond memories from my life in Lysterium, but everything changed when I met her."

Liv felt a prick of remorse fill her heart and worked hard to steady her voice. "Tell me about her."

For a brief moment, Lucian's face seemed to wash of its torment. He straightened, the deep crow's feet around his eyes, and the heavy indent between his brows seem to lessen in severity. His face brightened at the mention of her mother, giving Liv a glimpse of the once handsome man shining through. "She was the most beautiful creature I'd ever laid eyes on. I never imagined I'd fall in love with a human, but she stole my heart the moment I met her. She had this light in her that was so bright it illuminated everything, and she loved me. I brought her here once. It was as if she knew Lysterium, every detail. I found out that her mother had been here and told her stories. She said she never believed them to be true until the day I brought her."

"I know the feeling."

Lucian looked at her, surprised. "Are you human?"

"Yes—well, half. Go on."

He seemed fascinated by Liv. "I was going to propose to her. I had a ring, since that's the human custom. I promised her I would return after I dropped off the ship. I was already late coming home, because we had spent a month together, two weeks longer than I was supposed to stay. One perfect month. I planned to sell my ship to a colorful young man named Finnegan Riordan. I took him on as part of my crew for years, mentored him in the trade business, and taught him to sail Lysterium waters."

Liv's eyes threatened to spill over with tears. She tried her best to hide her emotion after hearing Finn's name. It was hard enough to face what she had to tell Lucian about her mother; she didn't think she could deliver the blow about Finn as well. Now wasn't the time, and for her, the loss was still too fresh.

Lucian didn't seem to notice Liv fighting back tears; he was stuck in the past for the moment and continued to talk. "I knew Finn would be thrilled about buying my ship and taking over the trade. He was so eager to have his own ship. I was equally thrilled, since it would allow me to live on Earth with Evelyn permanently. It wouldn't have been difficult to get a human job. We spent every moment together for that month, it was hard to leave her, but I was so excited. One last trip home, and my life was going to start—or so I thought. But on my way home, a bad storm hit, and my ship was lost at sea. That's how it happens, you know—ships that are lost on Earth get trapped in the Harbor. I didn't think I would survive the Sirens, I made it out." He looked down at his leg. "But not without loss."

Liv stared at the wooden post that bore into his dilapidated thigh. His flesh had long since healed over the wood, and two belt straps kept the wooden leg on. She wondered how painful it must have been to thrust an object into a missing limb and learn to walk on it. She shuddered at the terrible trauma he had been through.

"I washed up on the shore of the island, bleeding and weak, and things only got worse. There were creatures on the island—beasts—demons more like, I'd never seen before—and sailors driven mad. I hid in a cave most of the time, waiting for my death to come. I heard the creatures ripping apart sailors on the shore and heard other sailors fighting and killing. No one lived long, I imagine they were all human. I lost track of days and months at some point, but this went on the entire time I was there. I mourned when I heard their screams, but I couldn't save them. As less and less sailors were there, the creatures eventually stopped pacing the shores. I didn't know where they went to after that, so I stayed hidden, alone." He stopped for a moment, turning away from Liv.

She put a hand on his shoulder. "There was nothing you could do. You were wounded; it was a harsh reality. Don't let guilt fester in you, Lucian. You did what you had to do to survive. I can't imagine being alone that long, I would've been so afraid." She tried to comfort him, but the memories would never erase, and he would have to bear them for the rest of his life.

He put his bony fingers on hers and nodded.

"Lucian, can you look at me, please?"

With difficulty, he turned his face, and his eyes met hers.

"The woman you loved, Evelyn—"

His eyes widened, and the hopeful look on his face made Liv's stomach squirm. She suddenly felt terrified to tell him, but she had to. Maybe he would find some peace in knowing he had a daughter, or maybe not.

"Lucian, Evelyn was my mother."

Lucian studied Liv's face. "That would make sense, since I thought you were her. So, she met someone else and settled down. That's good." His tone was pained, but accepting.

For Liv, her mother's death was still painful, and choking the words out was difficult. "No." Liv steadied herself.

Lucian wrinkled his brow with apparent confusion.

Liv swallowed. "I'm sorry to be the one to tell you this. When I was young, she was murdered by Umaro."

If a heart ripping apart could have made a sound, Liv would have heard it. Tears slid down his hollow cheeks, and the angst was never more prevalent in his face.

Liv started to cry. "She didn't meet anyone else. I never knew my father, and I just recently found out that, well, *you* are my father. I came to find you."

The silence was deafening. As they stared at each other, with tears silently streaking their faces, it seemed as if the world stopped; everything was still, except for the crashing waves far below.

He spoke barely above a whisper. "How?"

"After you left, she found out she was pregnant. She wrote to you, but you were never seen again. She thought you left her. I didn't know anything about you, let alone that you were alive or a Lysterian, until my grandma died just recently. She left me a letter with these, explaining the little she knew." Liv handed Lucian the pictures. "I couldn't believe it, but when I saw your picture, well, my resemblance to you was undeniable. I don't know where to begin telling you about what has happened." She turned and rested her forearms on the worn wood railing and folded her hands. The words began to spill from her lips, "In short, Umaro murdered my grandmother. After that, she kidnapped Wes and I, and with the royals' help we were able to capture her and put her in prison. About a month ago, she sent me a letter saying she knew who you were and where to find you." The words were tumbling out in such a rush, "So I came back to Lysterium. It turned out to be a ruse to help her break out of prison. When Coralis, Wes, and I went to find you, I didn't know if you were even alive. But here you are, the only family I have left." She sharply inhaled, as she had spoken the last sentences in one hurried breath.

Lucian didn't speak. With a stunned look on his face, he touched the picture of the two of them near his ship. He traced his finger over Evelyn's face for a moment before handing the photo back to Liv. "Why would the red queen kill Evelyn? To what end? And how did you defeat her?"

"That's the confusing part—for me anyway. I'm in the Book of Prophecy, said to be the one destined to overthrow Umaro, of which I still have my doubts. She always seems to be miles ahead of us, and she's so strong. Finding out that you are Lysterian made my powers make a lot more sense. The only conclusion I can think of is that Umaro thought my mother was the one from the prophecy, but no one knows for sure why she killed my mom. Now she has escaped, and I've made a huge mess of everything." She looked down in shame. "Oh, and Wes—you know, the ruler of Elderwood, or whatever—we got married."

Lucian coughed to cover his surprise. "You married a royal!" His eyes were wide with astonishment. "My daughter? A royal?"

"It was pretty shocking to me too."

He moved closer to Liv and made a motion toward her, but hesitated. Slowly, Liv moved toward him. He touched her face and tucked her hair behind her ear. "I can see you have my eyes and chin—when I was in better health anyway."

Liv smiled, and they hugged briefly. His ribs jutted out, and his frame had deteriorated, yet she felt relief. She had a father, and he was holding her—something she'd always dreamed of but never thought possible. Many unanswered questions had been resolved the moment she'd found Lucian. They had found each other. At last, Liv knew the other side of her past, which hadn't made much sense until now.

Lucian let go and wiped a tear from his face with his thumb. He groaned with discomfort and rubbed the side of his neck. Many wounds and scars covered his body; they were older and scabbed, all but the one on his neck, which he was rubbing. It was recent—a still-seeping, long horizontal slice on the left side.

Liv tilted her head to see it. "That looks fresh. When did it happen? You're still bleeding a bit." Liv pulled out a tissue from her coat pocket and handed it to him.

Lucian dropped his hand, took the tissue, and nodded in appreciation. "It happened today."

Liv tensed. "Was it the man in the canopy?"

"No, that man was a mad sailor. He had been hunting me for a while, and yesterday he tried to kill me. This—" he dabbed his neck "—happened not long before you arrived. I was ambushed by a group of loathsome creatures. No doubt they were from Darcerion, and there was a woman with them."

Liv's stomach lurched, and she spoke slowly. "A woman? What did she look like?"

"The creatures held me down while she cut my neck. I thought she was going to kill me, but she just filled a small vial with my blood and released me. She seemed so pleased afterward. She even smiled. She was terrifying. She had intensely bright red hair and—" He stopped because of Liv's face.

She stared wide-eyed, her mouth slightly agape. She started backing up, still looking at Lucian, and then swiftly turned and started to run, letting out a shriek. "Wes!"

Lucian flinched as she disappeared into the darkness of the gardens.

Liv ran as fast as she could, still screaming for Wes. She made it halfway up the steps, when she crashed into him full force. She was thrown down the steps from the impact, and knocked hard onto the ground.

"Liv!" Wes ran down the stairs and helped her up. "Are you all right? What's wrong?" He looked over and spotted Lucian.

Liv was gasping. The fall had knocked the wind out of her. "Lucian—Umaro!"

"Liv, breathe."

She shook her head. "Can't. I'm freaking out. Umaro got to Lucian before we did. She took his blood!" She hunched over and clutched her side, trying to catch her breath from the fall. "She left him alive to buy herself time, so we wouldn't know she'd been there."

Wes, disconcerted, ruffled his hair. "That means she broke the curse, and she has her full powers back. And she has the Darkwater Book." He didn't say any more.

By then, Lucian was hobbling toward Liv and Wes. She was crouched down, hugging her knees, looking stricken. "Liv? What happened back there? Are you okay?"

Liv looked up with tears in her eyes. "It's over. She's won."

Wes, who had been deep in thought, pulled her back to a standing position and looked directly into her eyes. "She hasn't won yet."

"Who are you trying to convince, Wes? She broke the curse, she has all her powers back, and she has the Darkwater Book!"

Lucian raised his hand. "Will someone please tell me what's going on?"

Liv turned to him. "The woman who took your blood was Umaro."

Lucian gasped. "The red queen of Torr? Why would she want *my* blood? I only know her by reputation; I'd never seen what she looks like."

"She needed my blood to escape prison, but it cursed her, so she needed more to undo the curse. She couldn't get to me a second time, so she took it from you. We share the same blood. You're my father, the next best thing."

Wes interjected. "I have to go tell everyone right now. We need to come up with a plan before things get worse." He flew with great speed to the door and disappeared through it.

Lucian started to walk forward, when Liv stopped him. "This isn't your fight; it's mine. I'm the one who has to stop her. I have to find the answer. You've been through enough. I'm sorry. I have to go."

Lucian nodded, knowing he was useless in this situation. What did he have to offer now that he was broken? Although he was Lysterian and didn't age like humans did, he was no longer vital and strong. The Harbor had taken every toll from him but his life; he had nothing left. Liv ran up the steps and disappeared into the ship, and Lucian formulated a plan for himself. He sat in the garden, facing the sea, and tried to soak in the information he had learned about Liv and Evelyn and how the world had changed. He sat out there with his thoughts until the moon was starting to go down. Then, quietly, he went to the room he was staying in, unnoticed by anyone.

C HAPTER 23
Ashes

IT WAS EASY FOR LUCIAN to slip away with all the commotion over Umaro. He couldn't stay on Harp Isle anymore. He sought out Magnus with a specific potion in mind. His sadness was overwhelming, and it had been growing worse since the news of Evelyn. There was no place for him now. He had left the island, but the destitute malignancy of his emotional and physical state was like a prison. He'd thought he would die in the Harbor, and now, after all the long years of pain, he'd been rescued, but Evelyn was gone. He didn't know how to pick up the pieces of a broken life anymore.

Magnus didn't disappoint. He had what Lucian was looking for, but he was hesitant to give it to him. "Look, there's no turning back once you use it. If you were to change yer mind—"

Lucian interrupted politely. "I appreciate your concern, but I know what I'm doing. Thank you." He smiled, took the vial, and left.

His plan was to go to Earth. Being from Pyxis, he knew the fastest way to get to Earth would be through a portal, and the last he knew, there was an old one that wasn't used anymore near the giant clock tower in the market. He decided to walk there so he could enjoy the city one last time before leaving Lysterium. The sun was just peeking above the sea, casting a red glow over the city. Things had changed in the time he was at the Harbor, but some things remained the same, which was a comfort to him. As he reached the tower, and to his delight, the portal was still intact. He lifted his head, closed his eyes, and inhaled deeply, letting the salty air fill his lungs. He held his breath for a moment. His skin glowed red against the rising sun, while the cool breeze rustled his loose clothes. The sounds of the busy market and the lapping seawater against the dock gave him one last consolation. He lowered his head, opened his eyes, and stepped into the portal.

He had finally returned to the place where his great love was, as he had promised all those years ago. Lucian walked the cold streets, knowing the path he was taking, although he had only seen the house one time. He didn't know why he was going to Mona's, but he felt he needed to. When he arrived at the mansion, he picked the lock and pushed the door open. The creak of the door echoed in the foyer as he noted the dead flowers in the vase. It felt different from the way it had the last time he had been there. Everything had been so alive, as if the house were a person in itself. Now it was cold and lonely.

He walked toward a room off of the staircase—Evelyn's room. When he opened the door, everything was covered in dust, preserved like a tomb, and it was clear no one had entered the room in many years. He picked up a mirrored jewelry box on the vanity, revealing a square of clean wood void of dust. He opened the box, but what he was looking for was missing. As he left the room, he lingered in the doorway, taking in the room. He then made his way to the library. Looking around, he found an address book. It contained the address for Liv's apartment. He ripped the page out and put it in his coat pocket.

He wandered around the house slowly for a while, looking at all the pictures, until he found one that stopped him completely. It was of Evelyn and Liv. Liv couldn't have been more than three years old. Evelyn was laughing while Liv sprinkled flowers on her head. He picked up the frame, and a tear fell onto it. It was a life he'd missed, but they seemed happy. He slipped the frame in his pocket and headed for the front door.

Lucian's career had given him superb navigation skills; he found Liv's apartment easily enough. He flipped the torn address-book page over and began to write. When he'd finished, he slid the note under her door and left.

It was getting colder as he walked the long distance, he made his way through the trees, and the cemetery finally came into view. It was silent, filled with a stillness that calmed the air and quieted the mind. He searched for the gated area with Evelyn's family crest. The headstones were old. The gray of their stones was worn, some had moss covering them, and others were cracked with age, but all were dusted with powdered snow, giving the cemetery a monochromatic look. The black and white colors echoed how Lucian felt, old and as though leached of all color and vitality.

The rusty gate creaked as he opened it, and the sound echoed throughout. Snow crunched drearily under his feet. He stood in front of Evelyn's headstone, motionless for a few moments, and then he wiped the snow from the stone, taking extra time to sweep out all the engraved letters. "I never expected it to be like this. Maybe if I'd been there, I could have protected you. We could have been a family, the three of us." He started to cry and pulled the frame from his pocket. "I just don't know how I can be a father now. After all of this, after everything I missed, she deserves better than a ghost."

He knelt down on the plot, pressed his face against the headstone, and smoothed his hand along it. "I wish I could hold you. I wish I could rewind the clock and never get on that ship." He sniffed and took a deep breath. He leaned the frame against the headstone and then pulled Magnus's vial from his pocket and drank all of the contents in one quick gulp. "I'm sorry, Ev. I'm so sorry that all of this happened." He sobbed the words, "I've never stopped loving you; you were always with me. It's done. Now, maybe we can be together again."

From his foot, slowly moving up his body, he was turning to ash. He looked up at the gray sky. "I love you, Evelyn," he whispered as the ash enveloped him. Lucian had taken an incineration potion. The gentle breeze blew against his ashes, which were still in the form of a man, until they crumbled, spreading over Evelyn's plot, covering the framed picture, and rising into the air, becoming lost in the gray sky.

C HAPTER 24
The Outlook Is Grim

LIV HAD BEEN UP FOR so long, worrying and trying to figure out a plan, that she had nodded off for the last hour before finally falling asleep in a chair next to the fireplace. Coralis gently touched her arm, and Liv jolted awake.

"I'm sorry to wake you." Coralis said softly.

Liv was groggy. She noticed Coralis's face, and it made her straighten quickly into a seated position. "What happened! You've been crying?"

Coralis nodded. "Olivia, I need to tell you something that's going to be hard to hear."

Liv's breathing quickened. Part of her wanted to scream for Coralis to withhold the information, but the other part needed to know.

"I was summoned by Azrael today."

"The one who burned my eyes?"

"Yes, Azrael is the archangel of death."

Liv's face fell, and her heart sank into her stomach. She just knew, though she denied it with everything in her.

Coralis's captivating eyes glistened with tears. She sniffled a little in her delivery of the grim news, "It's—It's Lucian. He k-killed himself this morning."

Liv's eyes moved back and forth as she searched Coralis. She couldn't speak. She couldn't breathe. The room was spinning. Coralis caught her before she hit the ground. "Liv!" She gasped and called out, "Weston!"

Wes was in the room in seconds. "What happened to her?" He bent down and picked her up, cradling her head against his chest. He looked at Coralis, with widened eyes. "Weston, Lucian is gone. He killed himself this morning. I just told her, and she fainted." Her brow furrowed. "I'm sorry I had to be the one to tell her. Azrael called me to counsel this afternoon." She wiped a tear away and left the room abruptly.

This news was a blow to Wes. After everything they had risked and lost, nearly dying just to get to him, Lucian had committed suicide? His face turned red with anger. Liv had finally found her father, only to lose him right after. Had anyone even noticed Lucian wasn't there?

Liv stirred. "What happened?"

Wes looked down at her. "You fainted. Are you all right?"

She rubbed her head and remembered the news about Lucian. "I need to lie down, Wes."

"You're exhausted from all this stress. I'll carry you upstairs."

She touched his cheek. "I'm fine. I just want to rest. I'll come back down in a little bit." She stood up, brushed her hair out of her face with her hand, gave Wes's worried face a faint reassuring smile, and then headed for the upstairs bedroom.

She opened the door to the elaborate room. The afternoon light filled the space with soft beams of sun. She walked to the wall of windows, shut the curtains, and turned on the small light on the desk. She rubbed her eyes and sighed heavily. She should've had a million thoughts swarming her mind, but she felt numb. She was exhausted and stressed; her heart was troubled. This wasn't the first time her world had come crashing down, and she felt certain it wouldn't be the last, with the news of Umaro regaining her power. She felt dizzy again. She fell asleep so deeply she didn't even dream. She woke up to Wes sitting on the edge of the bed, gently rubbing her arm.

"Liv?" he whispered.

She startled awake, inhaling. "How long have I been out?" She was still half asleep.

"Not long. I'm sorry to wake you, but you need to eat something. You haven't had any food in a long time. You'll sleep better once you feed your body."

Liv was irritated. She wasn't hungry; she just wanted to sleep. However, as usual, he was right, and when she saw the plate he had for her, she suddenly felt half starved. She sat up and took the plate. She patted the bed for Wes to sit and started to eat.

"Wes, I need to go home." She noted his disapproval. "I know you think it's a bad idea, but I need this. I just need to be away from here for a while. It's too much."

"After all the fight to come here—" he sighed.

"I know. I'm sorry for putting you through all this. It seems pretty pointless with the outcome now." She rubbed her eyes. "I feel like every time I'm in Lysterium it's danger, and insanity, this doesn't feel like home, you know? I can't really de-stress here."

Wes lowered his eyes and slouched slightly "I don't want that feeling for you, but I rule a region here. What does that mean for our future?"

Liv had a jolt in her stomach "I'm not making anything definitive. I just need to go home for a little while and recharge. We don't have to talk about all that now. I know you're tied to Lysterium, I know how important that is. And of course, it makes more sense to live here since I have no family left—"

"Liv, I—"

She interrupted "It's okay. It is what it is. I'm just not up for that conversation fully, right now. Is that okay?"

Wes stood up and set her finished plate on the dresser. "Of course that's okay. We had so much happen since our wedding, we never really had to time to figure out the logistics. There will be time for that later. I suppose a few days on earth won't do too much damage. Umaro is in Darcerion; she probably won't attempt going to Earth right now. And I can be in contact with my family while we're there."

"Good. And I want to pick up Icarus from Eljene. I need to snuggle him. I need things to be normal for a few days. I miss my boy."

Wes smiled. "All right. When do you want to go?"

"Now."

Wes raised an eyebrow. "Don't you want to sleep first?"

"No. I'll sleep better in my apartment."

Liv packed up her things, put her shoes and coat on, and headed downstairs to meet Wes. He had gone down to tell everyone the plan. He had also sent one of his smoke birds to fetch Icarus, who teleported there, not long after. When Liv opened the bedroom door, her cat was standing there waiting.

Liv dropped her bag and screeched, "Icarus!" She scooped him up and hugged him for a long time. She buried her head in his fur inhaling his scent, which flooded her with a feeling of home and relief. "I missed you so much! I hope things weren't too weird with Eljene."

"It was interesting. I really like her, but I missed you."

Liv hugged him tighter. Icarus always made her feel better. Wes came upstairs and saw them reunited. He smiled and picked up her bag. Liv looked up at him and grinned. "I'm already starting to feel right again. You, Icarus, and my apartment—that's what I need. I'm ready to go."

When they arrived at the apartment, Liv almost burst into tears. She had longed for her old routine and normalcy amid all the chaos that had consumed her life recently. She hadn't put Icarus down since she'd first picked him up back in Pyxis. She walked upstairs and finally set him on the floor. He rubbed against her leg twice and went to his bed in the nook of the hall. She went straight to the bathroom, not noticing the small piece of paper on the floor.

Liv started the shower, brushed her teeth, combed through her hair, walked to the bedroom to set her coat and shoes down, and went back to the bathroom. Wes set her bag down on the floor and came up behind her in the bathroom. He kissed her neck and started to unbutton her shirt. She closed her eyes as he moved down her neck, kissing her shoulder. "That's nice," she said with a smile.

He turned her around and lifted her up onto the vanity. She weaved her fingers through his disheveled platinum hair and stared at his glacial blue eyes. "I wonder if we are ever going to have a normal life together."

Wes entwined his fingers with hers, bringing her hands between them. "Right now, we have to trust the prophecy. It's all we have."

Her smile faded. "What if it's wrong about me? What if I'm not really the one?"

The steam from the shower was fogging up the mirror behind her. Wes wiped his hand across it and gently turned her shoulders so she could see herself in it. "She's there. You just have to find her. You'll know when the time comes, and no one else can prove it to you until you do."

She turned back, and slid her hands up his shirt, moving her fingers upward against his skin. She felt the thickened gash on his ribs, and looked at all the scars he had accumulated from the Harbor on his arms and face. She lifted his shirt to look at the largest of the new scars, and sank into self-loathing, *she* had stabbed him and punctured his lung. Wes had suffered a lot of pain since she'd met him, and she feared it would only get worse. Her greatest fear was that something would happen that he couldn't be healed from. Then he would be gone. That had almost happened at the Harbor. She'd been about to kill him herself while under the Sirens' spell. There are some things a person couldn't be healed or saved from—like poor Finn.

Wes was an anchor for her. He kept her sane, and she loved him more than she'd thought possible. Umaro had taken everyone else Liv had ever loved from her. Although Umaro seemed to have a soft spot for Wes, as evidenced by her distress when the blood oath killed him, she was plunging deeper into darkness. Liv didn't know what Umaro would do, or if she would eventually kill Wes to hurt Liv.

Wes took Liv's face in his palms letting his shirt fall back down. "What's going on in there?" He searched her face.

She brushed her thumb over the dark, fresh scar below his eye from the Siren. His high cheekbone made it more noticeable. It was so close to his eye. She shook her head. "Too much. Don't worry about it. What I really want right now is a shower—and you." She smiled and finished unbuttoning her cardigan. Wes kissed her as he closed the door with a sweeping motion in the air with one hand.

After the shower, and some husband time, Liv slept for fourteen hours. She felt much better the next day. For now, in her mind, Wes was just her husband; he wasn't a magical royal from another world who was trying to stop a madwoman. Today they were just an ordinary married couple with a cat, doing ordinary everyday things, and she was happy for the first time in a long time. When she was ready for the day, she went downstairs. Wes was on the patio, pacing and talking to Amara through telepathy about any news regarding Umaro. Liv looked around her apartment, and saw a piece of paper near the front door, with a footprint on it. She put down the French press she was about to pour into a mug and picked up the paper.

She recognized immediately that it was a page from Mona's address book. She stared with concern, wondering how it had gotten there, and slowly flipped the page over.

Dear Liv,

I'm sure you have many questions, and to you, what I've done probably seems rather selfish. For that, I'm truly sorry. I should have died years ago, why I didn't, I'm not sure, but I never really came back from that island. Evelyn was what kept me going, fighting, and now that I know she's gone, trying to move forward just isn't an option for me. I don't know what your hopes were in finding me; I'm sure some part of you felt like you finally had a father. I wish I could be the father that you needed and deserved. I could never be that for you, because I'm barely even a man anymore.

You are a strong, kindhearted, and beautiful woman, just as your mother was. I'm proud to know that you turned out so wonderfully. I know there's so much more you wanted from me—answers—but there really is nothing more I can say, except that I want to be with your mother, and I can't bear the aftermath of what I've been through any longer. Life has not been fair to you, and what I've done isn't fair either, and for that, I'll be forever sorry. I hope someday you can understand. I feel confident in leaving you, because I know you'll be taken care of. You're married to a royal after all. For what it's worth, I'm proud of you.

I went to Mona's to retrieve my compass. I had left it with your mother, so she had a part of me while I went back to Lysterium. It wasn't there, so I'm hoping you already have it. I wanted to give it to you. When I was born, I was given that compass. If anything, it can serve as a family heirloom on your Lysterian side. It's a special compass, for it tells more than just direction; it navigates the heart. Perhaps it can help you in your journey to understanding your role in the Book of Prophecy and the future of Lysterium.

Thank you for rescuing me and for showing me kindness. Thank you for giving me one piece of joy in knowing I had a daughter through the misery and darkness I've been through. It's time for me to leave this life, and you should move forward and be happy. I'll be where your mother is buried, so both of us will never be too far from you. Good-bye, sweet Olivia.

All my love, Lucian

Liv dropped her hand with the letter in it, and it rested on her thigh. A part of her was angry. The hardships, the ordeal to find him, and the hope of having a living family member had all for been nothing. His act *had* been selfish. But another part of her felt sympathy and even empathy for him. If she had been in his place, would she have wanted to go on living after what he had been through? If Wes had died back in Umaro's castle, would she have been stable? She knew she wouldn't have. In fact, she probably would have been dead already, on a reckless vendetta. In some strange way, she felt as if she and Lucian finally shared something: passion. They both loved without restraint, and she couldn't be mad at him, no matter how much she wanted to be.

She put the note in her desk drawer in the living room. She walked up to the bedroom, pulled out her coat, and retrieved Mona's envelope and the compass. She pulled the pictures out and stared at them for a long time. She rolled the compass around in her palm and looked for any sign of help from it. *What did he mean it navigates the heart?* She hoped that maybe someday that part of his message would be less cryptic. For now, she placed the pictures on her vanity mirror and put the compass in her jewelry box.

Wes had come in, and he saw the mug on the counter and called up to her. She came downstairs and told him what had happened. He hugged her. "I'm sorry. Do you want to talk about it?"

"Not really."

"All right. My mother said that Umaro is still in Darcerion. From what she can tell, she will be gathering numbers. We lost our advantage with the curse, so now we have to figure out how to get ahead."

Liv let out a laugh. "That's the problem. It feels like she's about five hundred steps ahead of us at all times."

C HAPTER 25
An Unexpected Visitor

LIV AND WES HAD BEEN back, on Earth time, for almost a week. Umaro was still in Darcerion as far as everyone knew. Wes was reading the newspaper on the couch with Icarus on his lap while Liv made pancakes. They played cards, watched movies, sat and talked about little things, and just enjoyed being together at home. That night, Liv was lying against Wes on the couch, reading a book while he played with her hair.

He mindlessly wrapped her waves around his fingers in circular patterns, going over details in his head, trying to come up with solutions.

Liv leaned forward and turned toward him. "I was thinking."

Wes sat up straighter and focused on her instead of his thoughts.

"There has to be something to this locket. I think that's the next step we need to take; we need to find it. Maybe it has something to do with how I can defeat her."

Wes sighed and sat back again. "Liv, the locket was stolen during the wars. It hasn't been seen in two thousand years. I don't know if it *can* be found."

"Who stole it?"

He continued to curl her hair with his fingers absently. "I don't know. Umaro didn't know who it was. The night before she turned dark, someone went into her tent and took it."

Liv sat up and looked at him. "Did it have powers?"

"I never knew much about it, I was a boy then, but she never took it off. My mother would know more; they were extremely close before Umaro turned dark."

"Well, I think it's something we should explore, I need to talk to Amara when we go back." She lay back down against him.

He resumed playing with her hair. "The last place it was seen was Torr."

"Then we should start there." She yawned. "I really think this could be something, and I don't think she knows I know about it. I wouldn't have seen it in her memories if it wasn't important." She sat up again abruptly "I've just remembered, I saw it in the prophecy too! When I saw myself in the mirror, it was hanging next to my pocket watch—"

Wes tensed a little. "You never told me what you saw in the mirror"

"I saw myself, in the future. I don't know if it's what will happen, or just what could happen. But I saw us married, and that happened."

Wes stifled a smile "You saw us married?"

"Well I assumed, we were both wearing crowns, now that I'm thinking of it you had the chest tattoo," she paused "And the scar over your heart." She lowered her head. "I looked different though."

"How do you mean?"

"I was—wiser, it seemed. I had really long hair and a big scar on my eye. Also, I had the sword of the prophets with a piece of Umaro's hair wrapped around it. And the locket. It has to mean something. I think it's the key."

Wes stretched. "All right. We'll definitely look into it. I wish I could've seen that vision of you."

She put her book down, leaned back and closed her eyes.

Wes leaned his head back against the couch, resting his hand on her waist. "You know, as much as I was opposed to this little vacation, if you will, it's been nice," he said contently. "I haven't felt this relaxed in twenty years." He laughed.

Liv turned her head and opened her eyes. "Twenty years?" She laughed. "Old man."

A sheepish smile grew on his face as he lifted his head. He tickled her, and she flew off the couch with a squeal. He stood to chase her; his smile was warm and genuine.

"As fast and strong as you are, you gave up that easily?" Liv turned around, and her smile faded. "Wes?"

He was still standing by the couch. He didn't answer. He wasn't blinking, and one foot was still in the air from the step he was taking, frozen in place.

"Wes, what are you doing?" She walked over to him, touched his arm, and quickly pulled her hand away. He was cold.

"Wes!" She felt panic rising. She looked toward the other end of the couch, where Icarus had been. He was leaping off the arm, frozen in midair. Wes's knee had knocked a magazine over when he had stood, and its pages were fanned out, hanging midfall. She looked at the clock. The second hand gave one last tick and stopped. "What?" She heard a noise. Her whole body felt paralyzed. Someone was in the house.

In her peripheral vision, she saw a massive figure hooded in black. She tried to run, but before she could, a hand clasped over her mouth, and an arm wrapped around her waist, lifting her high off the ground. Her legs flailed, knocking into the dishes on the island. Her muffled screams of terror went unheard. The arms pulled her away from the island, hanging by her stomach, digging into her ribs. She writhed like a worm on a hook, helpless. Her feet desperately tried to find ground or anything to kick off of—any means of escape—but only met air. She clawed at the hand holding her mouth, still screaming and kicking, fighting as hard as she could. She looked at Wes, wailing through the hand and reaching for him. Her captor removed the hand over her mouth after she bit him.

"No! Help!" she screamed.

They were moving backward toward the stairs. Liv fought harder, clawing at the arm around her waist, her feet sliding down her captor's thighs, trying to find a grip. The hand that had been over her mouth rose in front of her eyes, gray and skeletal. She heard fingers snap.

"Wes!" she screeched.

Liv and her captor were gone.

Printed in the United States
By Bookmasters